MONTANA MAVERICKS

Welcome to Big Sky Country, home of the Montana Mavericks! Where free-spirited men and women discover love on the range.

THE REAL COWBOYS OF BRONCO HEIGHTS

The young people of Bronco are so busy with their careers—and their ranches!—that they have pushed all thoughts of love to the back burner. Elderly Winona Cobbs knows full well what it is like to live a life that is only half-full. And she resolves to help them see the error of their ways...

Brandon Taylor dated Cassidy Ware back in high school and it ended badly. A chance encounter with her ten years later leads to an impulsive one-night stand—and a pregnancy neither of them expected. He is ready to "take responsibility," but Cassidy isn't interested...unless he can prove he can be a true husband in every sense of the word!

Dear Reader,

Welcome back to Bronco, Montana! There's a big fancy wedding going on in Bronco Heights at the Taylor Ranch, and lone-wolf cowboy Brandon Taylor is getting tired of his brother's guests asking when *he's* going to give up the single life. The answer is *never*. He sneaks out of the reception to the stables for a little fresh air, but it seems someone else had the same idea. Cassidy Ware—his longtime nemesis since high school. But he and Cassidy get to talking. And kissing. And...

Suddenly, Cassidy is pregnant with Brandon Taylor's baby. A wealthy man used to getting what he wants, Brandon thinks Cassidy should marry him for the baby's sake. But Cassidy is holding out for love— something Brandon gave up on long ago...

I hope you enjoy Brandon and Cassidy's story. Feel free to write me with any comments or questions at MelissaSenate@yahoo.com and visit my website, melissasenate.com, for more info about me and my books. For lots of photos of my cat and dog, friend me over on Facebook: Facebook.com/melissasenate.

Happy reading!

Melissa Senate

The Most Eligible Cowboy

—

MELISSA SENATE

HARLEQUIN
SPECIAL
EDITION

Special thanks and acknowledgment are given
to Melissa Senate for her contribution to the
Montana Mavericks: The Real Cowboys of Bronco Heights miniseries.

HARLEQUIN®
SPECIAL
EDITION™

PLEASE RECYCLE

THIS PRODUCT IS RECYCLABLE

Recycling programs
for this product may
not exist in your area.

ISBN-13: 978-1-335-40803-7

The Most Eligible Cowboy

For questions and comments about the quality of this book,
please contact us at CustomerService@Harlequin.com.

Harlequin Enterprises ULC
22 Adelaide St. West, 40th Floor
Toronto, Ontario M5H 4E3, Canada
www.Harlequin.com

Printed in U.S.A.

Melissa Senate has written many novels for Harlequin and other publishers, including her debut, *See Jane Date*, which was made into a TV movie. She also wrote seven books for Harlequin Special Edition under the pen name Meg Maxwell. Her novels have been published in over twenty-five countries. Melissa lives on the coast of Maine with her teenage son; their rescue shepherd mix, Flash; and a lap cat named Cleo. For more information, please visit her website, melissasenate.com.

Books by Melissa Senate

Harlequin Special Edition

Dawson Family Ranch

For the Twins' Sake
Wyoming Special Delivery
A Family for a Week
The Long-Awaited Christmas Wish
Wyoming Matchmaker

Furever Yours

A New Leash on Love

Montana Mavericks: What Happened to Beatrix?

The Cowboy's Comeback

Montana Mavericks: Six Brides for Six Brothers

Rust Creek Falls Cinderella

Montana Mavericks: The Lonelyhearts Ranch

The Maverick's Baby-in-Waiting

Visit the Author Profile page
at Harlequin.com for more titles.

Chapter One

All Brandon Taylor wanted was to finish his small plate of delicious shrimp pot stickers, grab a bottle of champagne and sneak out of his brother's wedding reception for a little while. Half hour tops.

He stood in the parklike backyard of the Taylor family ranch on this warm, breezy early September evening, behind a pillar wrapped in twinkling white lights and festooned with tiny red roses, eyeing the best route to escape. The wedding had started at six and though it was now only seven thirty, it felt like two in the morning. The ceremony had been *a lot*. Or maybe just a lot for him. The look on his brother's face when his bride had started down the aisle had slammed Brandon in his chest. Had he ever seen Jordan look like that? Not just happy, not just proud, but as if he finally understood the meaning of life.

Then there were the vows. Goose bumps had unexpectedly trailed up Brandon's arms when Jordan repeated his vows and then said some of his own, the reverence in his brother's voice holding Brandon completely still.

"Dang," their brother Dirk had whispered from where they'd stood to the side of their oldest brother. "Double dang," Dirk's twin, Dustin, had agreed, wonder in his voice. Their sister, Daphne, was on the other side, in the bridesmaid lineup, tears misting her eyes, but Daphne had always been a softie. Plus, she had an engagement ring on her finger and would be next to get married so, of course, she was a little emotional at a wedding. What Brandon's excuse was for choking up, he had no idea.

Likely he was just happy for his big brother, a guy who'd always been a hero to Brandon. That was all.

Given the Taylor track record at marriage, Brandon hadn't thought any of his four siblings would make lifetime commitments. But there had stood Jordan, vowing to love, honor and cherish Camilla Sanchez till death did them part. There had stood Daphne, whose problems with their thrice-married, controlling father were legendary in Bronco, also believing in *forever* with that diamond ring twinkling on her finger.

Brandon *was* truly happy for both siblings, but he knew one thing about love: it didn't last. It just didn't have a chance.

So, add all that to the hundredth time a wedding guest had said, "I bet you're next, Brandon," and he was ready for a breather. A cousin had even added, "Good golly, Brandon, aren't you thirty-four? And still single? It's high time you settled down."

Brandon had politely smiled through it all until he just couldn't take it and had snapped at another cousin, a know-it-all lawyer from Butte with a gold wedding band on his hand, "Statistics speak for themselves. No thanks."

He'd gotten the stink eye from the cousin and a shaking tsk-tsk of the head from an aunt, and he'd been about to apologize for being the cynical smart-ass he could sometimes be when someone clanked a spoon against a champagne glass and everyone started chanting, "Kiss, kiss, kiss!" Jordan and Camilla stood in the center of the dance area, and his brother laid one on his new bride that even had Brandon kind of blushing. Cheers, wolf whistles and clapping followed.

Brandon glanced toward a stand of Rocky Mountain maple trees, his favorite grouping in the yard, the leaves already shimmering their yellow in the white lights hung around the perimeter of the reception area. Surely no one would miss him for a half hour. He'd already dutifully made small talk with at least a hundred of the countless guests. He'd complimented his dad's wife—number three—on the great job she'd done turning the yard of their family ranch into an outdoor ballroom, complete with all the strung lights and huge pink-and-red flower displays, penguin-suited waitstaff mingling with trays of appetizers and cocktails. He *had* managed to get into an argument with his father about his sister—something he'd promised himself to avoid—but any time Cornelius Taylor, who had a king complex, complained about Daphne, Brandon was going to defend her.

Their dad, whose beef cattle operation made him one of the wealthiest men in Bronco Heights, Montana, had a "my way or the highway" mentality, and when Daphne had chosen the highway, Cornelius had blown his stack. She'd moved out to start her own ranch, and a very different one, at that.

Daphne, a vegetarian of all things in a family of cattle ranchers, owned the Happy Hearts Animal Sanctuary, and Cornelius was always muttering that all the place was missing was shuffleboard for the old bulls and recuperating horses, plus the many dogs, cats and small furry creatures available for adoption. Between Daphne getting engaged and Jordan marrying Camilla tonight, poor Cornelius was out two of his five offspring to boss around, and that was his favorite pastime. Brandon loved his dad, but the man was a control freak.

And Brandon Taylor would never let anyone tell him what to do, when, or how. He was his own man and always had been.

He glanced around. Lots of smooching. Dancing cheek to cheek. Brandon had arrived solo at the wedding, but he'd been paired with a very attractive single bridesmaid in the wedding party. When she'd asked how many kids he wanted someday and he said he hadn't even thought ahead to whether he wanted beef or chicken for his dinner, she'd rolled her eyes at him and walked off. Now, as he spied a determined-looking middle-aged woman coming toward him with what looked like a calling card in her hand, he gave a fast smile and hightailed it from his hiding spot. He had at least twenty-five cards and slips of papers with the cell phone numbers and social media handles of single daughters, nieces, granddaughters, neighbors he'd be "a sure match with."

Doubtful. Love and Brandon had never mixed. Love and Taylors had never mixed, either, not that Brandon didn't wish his two siblings well. Daphne seemed to have found the real thing with Evan Cruise, and his brother Jordan looked so sickeningly happy right now, staring into his new wife's eyes while slow dancing to Frank Sinatra, that

Brandon really did have to hand it to him. The guy formerly known as He Who Would Not Be Tamed among the single women of Bronco had found his Ms. Right.

Brandon had spent the last few years making crystal clear to the women he dated that he would not commit. With his family history and not a single relationship working out for himself, Brandon put zero stock in romance and happily-ever-after, even when it was all around him—like at this wedding, a celebration of all things love and forever. Life had a way of not working out.

Cynical, sure. But true.

He popped the final pot sticker in his mouth, reminding himself to compliment his new sister-in-law on the catering her restaurant did for the wedding, then set the empty plate on a table. About to make off for the trees, he almost collided with a tiny elderly lady in her nineties.

Uh-oh.

There was no getting away from Winona Cobbs. No fast-talk, no evading. She had him pinned with her sharp gaze. Rumored to be mystic, Winona had a psychic shop at her great-grandson Evan's ghost tour business in town. Now that Evan was engaged to Brandon's sister, Winona was pretty much family. A psychic in the family sounded kind of scary. Not that he put much stock in mysticism, either, but with her long white hair, pale skin and mark-my-words look in her eyes, Winona Cobbs wasn't to be dismissed too easily. Plus, she deserved his respect. The lady had quite a family history of her own and had been through it all and then some.

"Brandon Taylor, you clean up well," Winona said, nodding as she looked him up and down through the rhinestone-dotted veil of her small purple cowboy hat. "Like a groom yourself in that spiffy tuxedo." She smiled wide and gave one end of her silver boa a toss over her shoulder.

He smiled back, shook his head and held up a palm. "No, ma'am. Not me. I'm more a lone wolf type."

"Oh please!" she scoffed. "I'll tell you what your problem is."

She sounded like his dad, he thought, his bow tie feeling tighter around his neck.

She leaned close. "Brandon Taylor, you don't know how to love. But I'll tell you something else. The universe has something in store for you. Oh yes sirree, it does."

Luckily for him, at the exact moment when he'd be expected to say something in response, two teenage girls approached Winona and asked if she'd do a reading for one of them. Apparently, the redhead had a crush on a boy who hadn't looked her way once during the entire reception.

"Oh, there are my twin brothers," Brandon said

fast, eyeing Dirk and Dustin by the bar. "Nice to see you again, Miss Winona."

She narrowed her eyes at him, but turned her attention to the girls, and he fled for the stand of maples, grabbing an unopened bottle of champagne from a passing waiter's tray. He loosened his bow tie and slipped through the trees, the strains of Ella Fitzgerald's "At Last"—the band's version—following him. He glanced beyond at the side yard. Empty. Two trees to the left and one up ahead, he'd be hidden from view and could then take the short path to the stables. Horses always had a calming effect on him. A twenty-minute breather and he'd head back to the wedding.

Brandon entered the stables and walked down to the far end, where he knew he'd find an over-stuffed chair with a little table beside it and a view of one of his favorite Appaloosas, Starlight, with her brown-and-white spotted back and flanks. But as he approached, he was surprised to see two long shapely legs crossed at the ankles, the feet bare, a pair of sexy silver high heels beside the chair. Who the gorgeous legs belonged to was a mystery, since the rest of the woman was hidden by a post.

Whoever she was, she clearly heard him coming because he heard a female voice mutter, "Not a moment to myself. Figures, right, pretty horsie?" and the legs pulled out of view.

Oh.

He knew that voice. Cassidy Ware.

She hated his guts. Had for over fifteen years. And *he* avoided her at all costs, which meant never going into Bronco Java and Juice, the shop she owned in town. A shame since everyone said she had both the best coffee in Bronco and the best strawberry-banana smoothies, a favorite of his. In all these years of avoiding the shop, he still hadn't gotten better at making a decent mug of coffee or getting the ratios right for his smoothies. Made him add to his list of grievances against Cassidy.

As he approached in the dim lighting, he passed Starlight's stall and there Cassidy was, sitting straight, arms crossed, staring daggers at him.

"Oh, it's you," she practically spat.

"Ditto," he said, narrowing his eyes at her.

Damn, she was pretty. Long, swirly blond hair past her shoulders, huge hazel eyes and delicate features. He'd always thought she looked like an angel. But she had a mind and mouth like the devil.

"Look, Taylor, I know your family owns the place, but I came out here to be alone, so…"

"*I* came out here to be alone," he countered. "And like you said, my family owns the place, so…"

She scowled. "You're as insufferable as ever. God, even on my birthday I can't catch a break."

He tilted his head. "It's your birthday?" He must

have known that at one point, but it had been a long time since he knew anything about Cassidy Ware.

She let a sigh pass over her glossy pink-red lips. "Happy thirtieth birthday to me," she sang.

"Happy birthday, dear Cassidy," he sang-added in his terrible baritone. "Happy birthday to you."

She laughed. "Well, thanks. But you can go now." She eyed the champagne. "Leave that, though, will you?"

Interesting. She'd also escaped the wedding to come out here, hiding from who knew what. He'd spotted her earlier in the kitchen, placing bite-size confections on a giant tray. His brother had mentioned that Camilla had hired Bronco Java and Juice to cater the nonalcoholic refreshments and desserts, including the wedding cake. Cassidy had probably been paid a small fortune. But she certainly didn't look happy. Then again, did she ever? Of course, it was possible that he associated her with a grimace because every time he ran into Cassidy around town, she crossed the street to avoid him. For all he knew, she could be the happiest woman on earth.

Except for her expression and slumped shoulders. Some birthday.

Oh, hell. He noticed a folding chair in the corner, grabbed it and then set it up beside her. "Tell you what. Because it's your birthday, you can have a slug. The rest is mine."

"You always were so thoughtful," she muttered, holding out her hand for the bottle.

He couldn't help but notice the lack of rings on her long, slender fingers. Not a surprise—first of all, Bronco was a very small town and he would have heard if she'd gotten married.

And second of all, she's completely *intolerable*, he thought, popping the champagne and handing her the bottle.

Some breather this would be.

Cassidy glanced over at Brandon, all six-feet-three of him stretched out in a well-fitting tux, bow tie askew, in a folding chair. His close-cropped dark hair made every angle of his gorgeous face visible, his strong nose and jaw, the intense dark eyes. Back when she'd had a mad crush on him as a freshman and had actually dated him for a few months, he'd been the cutest guy at Bronco High, and now he was so hot she could barely drag her eyes off him. His effortless hold over her had always been so unfair.

She took the bottle and lifted it in a silent *cheers*, then took a long sip. Then another. Ah, that was good.

Could her thirtieth birthday get any harder? The day had started out well enough. She'd been excited about tonight, taking part in the catering of such a fancy wedding at the Taylor Ranch. She'd been sure she wouldn't run into Brandon, nemesis for life, since the property was so big and there were three hundred and seventy-six guests. Everything had gone off without a hitch; she'd gotten so many compliments on her miniature pastries and tiny cookies and juice concoctions, which were available at the bar. But then word of her birthday had spread at the reception and the thirty-and-single nonsense had started.

Engaged and married former classmates had said, "Cassidy, be sure to line up for the bouquet toss so you can be next." Fake smile, giggle. Mariel Jones, a married accountant with two adorable twin toddlers, had said, "Oh, how sweet that you're catering the desserts. A big wedding like this probably pays months of your bills over at that little shop of yours."

Why were people so rude? And, dagnabbit, yes, this gig would help cover the slide into the cooler fall months and winter when business tended to slow down. April through early November, everyone wanted their mango-berry smoothies and ice mocha lattes and, of course, one of her decadent treats to go with them. Now, with the still beautiful early September weather, she had brisk business. But come December, folks wouldn't be venturing out as much in single-digit Montana temperatures. The fee for catering the Sanchez-Taylor wedding would be a nice boost, but she'd need more where that had come from.

And despite the great gig, she couldn't help but look around at all the accomplished, wealthy guests and wonder why she hadn't been able to make her goals come to fruition. Yes, she had her own business, and it was popular in Bronco Heights. But back when she'd been twenty-five, full of grit and determination, she'd made a business plan that had impressed Bronco Bank and Trust enough for the small loan she'd taken out to open the shop. She'd intended to have a chain of Java and Juices across Montana to start, including in city hotels like down in Billings. But, nope, five years later, at age thirty, everything was exactly the same. Cassidy was grateful for what she did have, but she'd really thought she'd be able to expand by now.

"Remember the bets we made?" Brandon asked, taking the bottle of champagne for a long slug and then handing it back to her.

She gaped at him, shocked *he* actually remembered. They'd been boyfriend-girlfriend for a few months when she'd been a freshman and he a big-man-on-campus senior. Between her mom giving her a hard time about dating a boy "who is too old for you and very likely used to getting *anything* he wants, given his family name" and the girls throwing themselves at him, she and Brandon hadn't really had a chance back then. She was constantly jealous of the older girls flirting with him and his friendliness back.

Once, toward the end, she'd accused him of standing her up for a date and catching him with another girl in the library, and then realized she'd made the mistake—the wrong day and the girl was Brandon's lab partner and already engaged to her own high school sweetheart. It had all just been bad timing back then and she'd been too young for Brandon Taylor in every way. She'd been in over her head and had broken up with him. But then he'd told everyone he'd broken up with her and, for some immature reason, that had rankled. She'd made a fuss, he'd shrugged, and they'd been antagonistic toward each other since, throwing little barbs that didn't really sting.

She'd tried to avoid him since, impossible in a town like Bronco, so the times they did run into each other, they'd just pretend they didn't see each other.

She thought back to that final day of their romance, the back-and-forth arguing in a back stairwell at Bronco High, Cassidy saying there was no way they'd make it as a couple to the end of the day, let alone the week. Brandon had agreed. That was when they'd flung their insult bets at each other.

"You'd bet that I'd be on my sixth child at age thirty," she said. "Well, I'm not even on number *one*. Hell, I don't even have a man in my life."

He stared at her and seemed about to say something, but didn't, just accepted the champagne bottle back from her and took another swig before handing it back. "And you'd bet that I'd be on my third marriage." He laughed, but his big grin soon faded.

"Instead, we're both single, no kids, hiding out in the stables during your brother's wedding. Whodathunk?" she asked.

"Gimme back that bottle," he said with a smile.

But she could see he was lost in thought and she wondered about what. An ex-girlfriend who'd gotten away? His own unfulfilled goals?

What *were* his goals, though? He was from the richest family in town, worked at Taylor Ranch in some cowboy-meets-executive capacity, and had everything he'd ever wanted. If Brandon Taylor wanted to be married, he would be.

"Why *are* you here?" she asked, surprised that she really wanted to know what had driven him from the wedding.

"The usual in-your-face questions from relatives I haven't seen in months or years," he said, his dark eyes on her. Then he looked toward the pretty horse in the stall across from them. "And my dad, as usual. One conversation with him and I need to decompress."

"Yeah?" she asked, her own father coming to mind. He'd left her mother—and her—when she was just shy of her first birthday. *I'm really sorry, but I'm just not cut out for marriage or fatherhood*, the cowboy had written in a note. He'd sent her mom money and a birthday card every year for Cassidy until she was eight, when he'd either completely forgotten she existed or had been just done with all that. Right or wrong, Cassidy had kept her distance from good-looking cowboys.

Brandon Taylor might not have to get his hands dirty, but he was a cowboy through and through. Mega rich made it worse. The entitlement and arrogance.

"He makes life on the ranch almost unbearable," he said, staring down at the floor. "You'd think trying to boss his three brothers—all equal partners in Taylor Beef—would keep him satisfied. But no, he has to try to control his five adult children." He shook his head and took another drink of the champagne, then passed it back. "Lately I've been thinking about what I really want out of life."

She stared at him, surprised he'd opened up. She didn't have experience with a controlling dad, of course. Her late mom had always been so busy trying to make ends meet that she'd given Cassidy a lot of responsibility to make the right choices. Cassidy always had. "Yeah, me, too. I mean, I know what I want. I just can't seem to make it happen."

"Those six kids?" he asked. "A husband?"

She narrowed her gaze. "I was referring to my

goals for Bronco Java and Juice. I thought I'd have expanded by now. But it's just the one small place." She shrugged, taking another drink of champagne, then handing it over to him. She truly wasn't caught up in being thirty and single. Marriage wasn't on her mind. Maybe because she'd never found the right guy. She'd had relationships, but one of them always left. Sometimes she thought her heart just wasn't in the idea of marriage. She'd been too young to witness her mother's heartache at being abandoned by her child's father, but she'd grown up with her mom's dictums. *Never depend on a man... Make your own way... Be independent... Don't expect anyone to rescue you. If you get in trouble, rescue yourself.*

So here Cassidy was, Miss Independence. With not as much to show for it as she'd planned.

"I really did like you back in high school," he said suddenly, sliding his gaze to hers. "Sorry I acted like an idiot. You did dump me and I wanted to save face."

Cassidy smiled. She wasn't about to tell him how much she'd liked him then, that he was her first love and that she'd never really gotten over him. Yes, Brandon Taylor had been a golden boy. But a smart one who'd worked hard for good grades, who'd tutored classmates for free in math, his best subject, who'd been friendly to everyone instead of a stuck-up jerk like a few of his teammates on the football and baseball teams. He'd defended the picked-on from bullies. And the way he'd talk about horses, his admiration of them and knowledge and intention to make them his life's work at the Taylor Ranch, had held her rapt. She used to ask him about his family and it had taken her a while to realize he only talked about his three brothers and sister, never his parents, who were clearly a source of agita. Those times she'd seen Brandon in town over the years? The words *unfinished business* always echoed in her head along with the red alert to avoid him.

"Well," she said, feeling a little Brandon-size crack in her heart widen, "an apology fifteen years in the making. I'll take it."

He laughed and passed her the bottle, which she raised to him and then drank from before passing it back. There wasn't much left.

"So about our bets," she said. "You're supposed to be on wife number three. Did you just never meet the right woman?"

He leaned back in his chair, his eyes moving to the Appaloosa, then back to Cassidy. "Don't much believe in it, I guess. Marriage hasn't exactly worked out too well for my parents—my dad's the one who's been married three times, though he and Jessica do seem happy. For now. And my mom? Haven't seen her since she left when I was five."

She almost gasped. She hadn't known any of

that. Brandon rarely talked about his parents back when they were dating. "I never knew my dad. And my mom never got married, which had once been a dream of hers. She fell in love with a ranch hand who sweet-talked her, and he left before I turned a year old. She kept asking where her ring was, and he kept saying he was saving up to afford a diamond worthy of her, with the next purse he won. He left instead. So, to be honest, I'm not much interested in marriage myself. Maybe I don't believe in it, either. I don't know anymore."

"Well, aren't we a pair," he said, tilting the bottle back. He handed it to her. "I saved you the last few sips."

She smiled. "Huh. I'd sarcastically called you thoughtful earlier, but you do seem to be just that."

"Not the bad guy you thought I was the last fifteen years."

"No," she said, finding herself leaning toward him just a bit, her gaze on his mouth. She'd kissed those lips many times ages ago. She remembered exactly how every nerve ending in her body had lit up when he'd held her close. That was Brandon the teenager. Brandon the man? Whew. She let her eyes travel down his long, muscular body in that black tux. Maybe *too* much man for her. Too much cowboy. He might be a good guy in general, but she'd seen him with a lot of different women over the years, one prettier than the next. Just last week she'd spied him through the window in Bronco Brick Oven Pizza with a gorgeous redhead. "When it comes to women, I'm sure you haven't changed a bit, Brandon Taylor."

He smiled that dazzling smile of this, the one that had always made her forget where she was—and all rational thought. "All I know for sure about you is that you're as beautiful as ever, Cassidy Ware."

Maybe she'd needed a compliment tonight on her thirtieth birthday. Because she was suddenly warming to Brandon. A little too much. She couldn't stop staring at his lips.

"What did we bet?" he asked. "I mean, what was the winner and loser supposed to get? That I actually can't remember."

She grinned. After they'd made their bets, she'd realized they were really just proclamations without anything to win or lose, and she'd demanded he eat his words if what he said about her didn't come true. "You said, and I quote, 'Fifteen years from now, whoever wins their bet gets bragging rights. Whoever loses has to wallow in being wrong. And if we both end up wrong, we'll have to kiss and make up and then go our separate ways forever.'"

"Well, we were both wrong," he said, holding her gaze, which dropped to her lips, then back up to her eyes. For a moment, she caught him slide a glance along her silky pale-pink cocktail dress.

Kiss and make up. Kiss and make up...

Before she could even blink, the bottle was on the floor, empty, and they were kissing, Brandon's hands in her hair, her hands splayed against his chest, moving up to his neck and to his chiseled face.

He pulled back slightly. "Tell me to go back to wedding. Or we might do something you'll probably regret. I *haven't* changed a bit. And we've had way too much to drink, Cass."

She liked how he used to sometimes call her Cass.

"We have," she agreed, the intoxicating scent of his cologne enveloping her. "But I don't think I'll regret anything."

Yes, she was tipsy. But it was her birthday and she'd been feeling sorry for herself not an hour ago. A secret birthday rendezvous with the man she'd never forgotten? The one who'd gotten away? *Finished* business after all these years?

"Me, either," he whispered. "But that might be the moment talking for both of us. You sure about this?"

He looked at her, his dark eyes probing and sincere instead of flirtatious and glib, and she knew he was giving her another moment to come to her senses.

She grabbed the lapels of his tux and kissed him hot and heavy on the lips. She would not regret this.

After all, tomorrow, all kissed and made up, they'd go their separate ways—forever.

But tonight? She *needed* this.

Chapter Two

Oh, yeah! Cassidy thought, eyes closed, back arched, lips ready for more. *Happy birthday to me!*

She opened her eyes when she realized she was wasting precious seconds of not looking up close and very personal at Brandon. She'd already unbuttoned his fancy white shirt when they'd moved into an empty, clean stall, and he'd flung the garment into a heap by the door.

Her gaze roamed over his gorgeous face, down the strong cords of his neck to his magnificent rock-hard chest and farther down to where a line of soft dark hair disappeared into the waistband of his tuxedo pants.

Brandon kissed her lips, her forehead, her neck as both of his hands reached behind her to unzip her dress, and she shimmied out of it. The straw under her was both soft and rough, which was fine with her.

She hadn't been expecting anyone to see her in her sexy pale pink lacy bra and matching undies tonight, but she was darn glad she'd worn them.

"Oh, Cassidy," he breathed, looking her up and down, down and up. "You are still so damned beautiful."

"You, too," she whispered, taking his face in her hands and kissing him, softly, passionately, and then with all the desire coursing through her body.

He let out a groan and his fingers were suddenly inside her bra, which was then quickly removed, his mouth on her breasts, her hands in his hair. She was kissing his neck when she felt her undies being inched down her hips. They could not come off fast enough.

As he kissed his way down her stomach, she almost screamed with pleasure before she remembered, barely, where she was. She practically had to bite down on her fist.

She reached for the button on his pants and the zipper, which elicited another groan from Brandon. In moments they were naked on the hay, this man she'd never been able to forget lying on top of her. She heard him grab his pants and take something out, followed by the unmistakable tear of a condom wrapper.

And then he looked at her, his dark eyes intense, before he kissed her with so much passion she had to have him inside her, one with her, immediately.

"Cassidy," he whispered. "You're everything."

I'm everything, she thought tipsily and happily. *I'm everything to someone*... And not just someone. Brandon Taylor, still special to her after all these years, no matter what she'd said or thought.

But suddenly she couldn't form another thought. Because for the first time ever, Brandon Taylor was making love to her. And the reality was even hotter than her traitorous fantasies since her school days.

"You have a piece of hay in your hair," Brandon said on a smile, reaching to pluck it out.

Cassidy grinned. "You, too." She grabbed it from near his ear and tossed it on the floor.

Being with Brandon, even though they were tipsy, was like nothing she'd ever experienced.

It wasn't just the insane levels of passion. But the unexpected tenderness. The way he'd stop for a second and just looked into her eyes, gently holding her face. Like that old song said, it was in his kiss. It was in everything Brandon had done to her. And she'd given it back with everything she'd had.

Now they lay on the floor, the scratchy hay not exactly Egyptian cotton sheets, but she couldn't be any more comfortable or relaxed. She could lie there forever. They both were looking up at the ceiling, at the wood beams of the barn with the dangling electric lanterns, and as if he felt exactly the same way she did, he clasped her hand.

He'd said he hadn't changed, but he sure had. She could tell just in the way he held her hand, a silent acknowledgment of *something*. Though, of course, they hadn't had sex back in high school for her to make any comparisons, but there hadn't been much in the way of poetic gestures back then.

"Well," he said, turning his head to face her before letting go of her hand and suddenly sitting up. "I guess we'd better get back to the wedding or someone might send a search party for us." He reached for his white shirt and slipped it on, then found his bow tie half buried in the hay.

Dismissed. Could the splash of water over her head feel any icier?

She forced a fake chuckle and reached for her dress, suddenly feeling very exposed. She turned and put on her bra and undies, then slid the dress over her head and popped up, dusting herself off.

"Do I look like I was rolling around the floor of a barn?" she asked, trying to make light.

He studied her for a second. "No. You look absolutely beautiful, as always. No one would ever guess what went on here."

I barely would, she thought, turning away so

he wouldn't see whatever strange expression was on her face. Disappointment. Embarrassment—for wanting more from him right now.

A half hour ago, she'd liked how earnest he could suddenly be, the sincerity in his voice moving. Now, a chill ran up the nape of her neck. This was Brandon Taylor. He could make you feel like the only woman in the world and then, a second later, remind you who he really was when it came to relationships.

A man who wanted to get the hell away from said woman and back to the wedding he hadn't been able to escape from fast enough.

That she really was slightly singed over this made her feel even worse. Stupider. What had she expected or wanted? Brandon to magically announce he was madly in love with her and carry her back to the wedding, where they'd dance every dance?

No, of course not. But something more than *wham-bam-thank-you-ma'am,* which was exactly what this felt like.

Oh, stop it, Cassidy, she told herself. *You're not Cinderella. He's no prince.* She spied her shoes—one wasn't lost on the castle steps, she hadn't gone from her pretty dress to tattered rags—and slid her feet into them. *This is exactly what you both set it up to be and he even made double sure you were in.*

So rescue yourself, she heard her mother say.

She was feeling a little bruised, so she'd simply go get happy and enjoy her thirtieth birthday. Go back to the wedding, listen to people compliment her on the gorgeous wedding cake that she knew would be scrumptious and bring in tons more business with future wedding cake orders. Have her prime rib dinner, dance a few dances with friends, and then go home.

And forget about Brandon.

Nothing to see here, nothing to be mad about.

"Well, well," she said as lightly as she could. "We made good on the bets. We kissed. We made up. Now we go our separate ways."

"Forever," he added.

She turned her head so suddenly to stare at him that she almost gave herself whiplash. *Forever.* Well, she knew where she stood with him.

He was dressed, too, now, but his bow tie was crooked, so she straightened it, aware that his eyes were on her. "Cassidy, I—"

She waited. "You what?" she asked when nothing else seemed to be coming.

"That was really something," he said, holding her gaze for a moment.

She felt a pang in her chest. What the hell was wrong with her? Why did she seem to be expecting something else from Brandon Taylor? Come on, Cassidy!

"Yeah, it was," she said, running a hand through her hair for more hay pieces.

"Shall we?" he asked, gesturing toward the high wooden gate of the stall.

There is no we, she wanted to scream. Instead, she calmly opened the door and walked out, then back along the long aisle of the stables and into the refreshing night air.

The last thing she needed was for anyone to notice her slipping into the yard with Brandon. She needed to keep this their little secret. "Well, I'll just scurry up ahead. Bronco is a small town and we don't want to be the big gossip of the wedding. Everyone knows we're supposed to hate each other."

"Actually, Cassidy, if people think we're a thing, maybe they'll stop telling me all about their single daughters, nieces and third cousins once removed and handing me phone numbers and cards."

"Yeah, that's gotta be rough," she said with a roll of her eyes. This was exactly what she needed. More of the Brandon Taylor she expected, the guy she always figured he was.

He nodded earnestly, adding to her ire. Perfect.

"Well, bye," she said and slipped off her heels again, grabbing them in one hand and dashing for the stand of majestic trees that would lead into the backyard where the reception was being held. Pressing a hand against the bark of a maple for support, she put her shoes on, lifted her chin, and came through the trees.

The good news was that the yard was the size of a football field, the reception area half of that, a vast space crowded with guests standing and chatting and enjoying refreshments. No one seemed to notice her as she slipped into the scene. The band was playing an old Bee Gees song. Cassidy headed to the buffet table, where she piled a plate with enough hors d'oeuvres to combat the effects of the champagne. She ate a smoked salmon crostini just as Brandon came through the trees.

Goose bumps trailed up the nape of her neck. Damn it. They'd just been as intimate as two people could be and now they were back to acquaintances. She didn't like how that felt one bit. She hadn't been intimate with a man in almost a year until now, but instead of feeling all energized and *yeah-I-needed-that*, she felt…alone. Cassidy and casual sex had never mixed.

At least she and Brandon had a truce, the old cold war settled. So now what? They'd politely smile if they ran into each other in the grocery store? Did Brandon Taylor even buy his own groceries? Probably not.

But he could finally come into Bronco Java and Juice, a place she'd long suspected he'd avoided because of her. Good. She could use his business. God knew the Taylor Beef boys didn't worry about the price of triple espresso lattes. Then again, she had a feeling Brandon would keep avoiding her, just for a very different reason this time.

She had no doubt there were many women in Bronco he took pains not to run into.

Cassidy ate a miniature mushroom empanada and watched as woman after woman chatted up Brandon as he moved through the crowd. Lots of cheek kisses. Lots of manicured hands running up his arms for no good reason. And there was Brandon Taylor's dazzling smile, loving it, no matter what he said about the rough life of having phone numbers thrown at him all night.

Now Sofia Sanchez, the bride's very attractive sister, whom Brandon had once dated, walked over to him and kissed his cheek, and they were both laughing at something.

Cassidy narrowed her eyes at them.

She knew what this awful feeling was. Jealousy. And she didn't like *that*, either.

She turned away and popped another tiny appetizer into her mouth. Dinner would be served at eight, her cake at nine. Once the cake was served, she could probably sneak out and head home—and hide under the covers till the morning light and a new day that would make this all feel like a dream.

Go our separate ways forever...

"May I have this dance?" said a familiar deep voice.

She whirled around to find Brandon holding out his hand. This was the opposite of avoiding her. Interesting.

Cassidy was so surprised that she reacted before she could think it through. She put her empty plate down and took his hand. He led her to the edge of the dance floor and they slow danced to the band's version of a Kacey Musgraves song that Cassidy loved. Brandon held her close and, with her eyes closed for a few moments, she was transported back to the stables, back to when they were one. All too soon, the song was over and Brandon was being called away for "extended family photos" with the bride and groom.

Completely off-kilter, Cassidy watched him head off with the group, taking a path that led to the front of the luxe log mansion. She could still smell that delicious cologne of his.

"Oooh, I thought you two hated each other," whispered a female voice from behind her.

Cassidy turned to find her friend Callie Sheldrick holding a small plate with a few hors d'oeuvres, her brown eyes wide with curiosity.

Cassidy bit her lip. "We ran into each other is all. A dance for old times."

"I thought old times were bad, though," Callie said with a gleam lighting her face. "You haven't had a good thing to say about Brandon since I've known you."

"He's a good dancer," Cassidy said.

Callie narrowed her eyes and grinned. "Something in the air between you two?"

Cassidy sighed. "Probably not. He's Brandon Taylor. Ultimate ladies' man."

"Eh, they're only ladies' men until they fall in love." Callie wriggled her eyebrows and popped a bite-size bruschetta in her mouth.

Cassidy took in that golden nugget. She supposed that could be true. Not that Callie had much experience with players, lucky for her. Her friend had fallen hard for Tyler Abernathy—anything but a ladies' man—a widowed rancher with an adorable baby daughter, and now they were a committed couple.

The band started playing a Frank Sinatra song and Callie was pulled away by her boyfriend, Tyler, for a dance. The song was almost over when Brandon reappeared and, once again, Cassidy was in his arms.

After the song, she would tell him to turn his attention elsewhere.

"Look, Cassidy," he said. "You probably expect the worst from me and I don't want to live up to that, so I'm going to be very honest."

She pulled back a bit to look up at him. "Okay," she said, bracing herself. She wanted honesty. She needed the second splash of cold water on her head.

"We had a pretty serious conversation earlier

about how we both feel about marriage…" he began. "Neither of us is interested in all that, right? I just don't believe in commitment. That way, I don't hurt anyone, either."

"And you're telling me this because…?"

"Because for the twenty minutes I was away from you, I wanted to be back with you," he said. "I have a thing for you, Cassidy Ware."

She laughed despite herself. He wanted her to a point. Was that what he was saying? Unbelievable.

"And so I'd like to propose a possible arrangement," he added, "if you're interested."

She could feel the smile slide off her face. Oh, Brandon. She sighed inwardly, exhausted, and it wasn't even eight o'clock at night.

"Let's see each other," he said. "Date. With no strings. Just two people enjoying themselves and each other. Like earlier in the stables."

Yup, this was exactly what she'd expected of Brandon Taylor. "I don't think so. But thanks for your interest."

"I *am* interested, Cassidy. And, really, why not? We both want the same thing—no ties. And we're clearly good together. So let's have all the good parts of a relationship without the stuff that invariably mucks it up."

She'd said that, that she didn't believe much in marriage. But was that really true? She wasn't sure. She might not think much of relationships working out, given her family's past and her own track record, but that didn't mean the idea of a no-strings relationship held much appeal. There was just something…empty about it.

"Well, think about it," he said.

She wouldn't. But, for a moment, she pictured the two of them in her bed. Why was her body such a traitor? She stood there, looking at him, and yes, she wanted to be kissing him. *Could* they have a no-expectations fling until it ran its course? They'd get each other out of their systems. Maybe that was what this was about. The unexpected opening up in the stables. The rendezvous in the stall. The dances. A few weeks of dating and they'd fizzle, and then they truly could go their separate ways. Forever. With no one getting hurt.

It wasn't like she'd fall in love with Brandon Taylor. Not with what she knew about his romantic history. She had big plans and ideas for her future, all involving Bronco Java and Juice. That was her focus right now. Meeting her goals—which didn't include a serious relationship.

"What's your cell number?" he asked, taking out his phone. "I'll text you a 'hi' right now so you'll have my number. Call or text anytime. Really. Any. Time."

She recited her number and, in moments, her phone pinged. "I'll sleep on it," she told him, but she wouldn't give it a moment's serious thought.

Flings could be fun if everything lined up. But there was too much history between her and Brandon, too much...*there*. Cassidy couldn't quite explain what that *there* was, exactly, but he wasn't just some random hot guy. Or a guy she didn't have feelings for. Her unexpected disappointment at the way she'd felt dismissed at the stables came flooding back. The sex over, there had been no conversation, just one clasp of the hands that she'd foolishly read way too much into. And then, *Well, I guess we'd better get back to the wedding or someone might send a search party for us.*

That was what being involved with Brandon would be like. Cassidy just wasn't cut out for that. Maybe if she didn't care—again, about *what* exactly she didn't know. But she did care.

He was pulled away yet again—more family pictures. Then it was time for dinner, so everyone took their seats. Brandon was at the family table.

Cassidy had been invited to the wedding by the bride herself, who'd been so kind to offer her the job of catering dessert. She checked her table number. Fourteen. She was far, far away from the family table, which was a good thing. She needed a break from Brandon Taylor. And she also needed that prime rib to sober her up even more. But as she headed for her table, which seemed to be filled with singles, she felt eyes on her and, when she glanced around, she saw the very elderly Winona Cobbs,

with her purple cowboy hat and snazzy silver boa
around her neck, staring at her with a strange smile.

Cassidy felt a chill go through her. Winona was
psychic. Everyone knew that. She had her own little
shop, Wisdom by Winona. Maybe Cassidy would
stop in sometime and get herself a reading. Right
about now, she could use a look into her future.

A few days later, Brandon sat at his desk in his
home office on the first floor of the family ranch,
trying to focus on the spreadsheet of numbers and
accompanying graphs. Brandon was an executive
vice president at Taylor Beef, which had its own
office building, but he'd stayed close to home since
the wedding. Since Cassidy. Right now he was supposed to be analyzing projected third-quarter sales
figures, but all he could think about was her.

Thing was, his mind wasn't on what it was usually on when he thought about a woman he was
very attracted to. Usually, he'd go over every de-
lectable detail of their time together in anticipation of the next time. That would have him calling
and texting. Instead, he was thinking about Cassidy herself. The girl he remembered—smart and
opinionated and full of ideas and plans for herself.
The woman she was now—a surprise. He hadn't
expected to feel so…connected, as if they were on
the same plane, same page. He'd thought they'd be

like oil and water and instead they were like milk and cookies.

He could count on one hand the number of times he'd felt like that about a woman he was dating. Three times, to be exact.

Marley O'Kane's beautiful face appeared like a scary mask in his mind's eye. The former Miss Mid-Region Montana who "couldn't afford to pay for her gravely ill, beloved granny's cancer treatment" turned out to be a grifting liar. "Granny" was really a boyfriend in perfect health with a gambling addiction and a loan shark after him. Marley was a decent actress who'd actually studied up on Brandon to win him over because he was a Taylor and she'd thought her model-like looks would earn her some blank checks. He'd been twenty-two and about to write that first check to Marley until his sister had sat him down and reported seeing Marley and another man all over each other at an Italian restaurant. A look into her background had revealed everything.

It had taken two years to get past his stupidity and gullibility and to let himself feel something again for a woman he was dating. Didi Philbin might not have been a duplicitous cheat like Marley, but after six months, she'd broken up with him for someone else, and he'd been blindsided and more damned hurt than he'd admitted to anyone.

He'd let a good few years pass before he'd fallen

for another woman, but he'd apparently had so many walls up that she'd told him being in a relationship with him was like being involved with a brick wall and that she'd had enough of trying to break through. His first reaction was that he'd work on it, he'd *try*, but not one brick dislodged and the lady had moved on.

So Brandon had stuck to flings and short-term romances where his lack of interest in commitment was stated up front. No one had gotten under his skin in a few years now, and Brandon found he liked it that way. There was something peaceful about it.

Except now he couldn't get Cassidy Ware out of his head. And that wasn't a good thing. Between his track record and his family history, he'd never commit and he'd never marry. His father had plenty of offspring to carry on the Taylor name. Jordan and Camilla would likely be giving Cornelius a new generation of heirs in no time. The way Brandon saw it, people either walked out on you or disappointed you or operated conditionally. And he was certainly no different or better than most. Ask any of the women he'd dated the past few years, many whom had deserved better than they'd gotten from him.

So in the few days since their night together, he hadn't gotten in touch with Cassidy. Not a word. That didn't sit right, but every time he grabbed his phone with the intention of sending a lighthearted text, he put it back in his pocket. And he felt all unsettled. Their last conversation had been about casual sex. A no-strings affair. Cassidy had agreed to "sleep on it," though he'd known full well she'd tell him to jump in a lake. Of course, she hadn't called or texted, either, to give her answer. So there was Brandon's "no." That was a good thing.

We kissed and made up and went our separate ways. Forever.

The idea of that—the word *forever*—left him weirdly unsettled, too.

He should just continue on, focus on work, and in a week or two, he'd barely remember the night in the stables. The Cassidy question settled somewhat, he picked up the printout of graphs on the quarter's numbers.

Before he could even attempt to concentrate, Brandon heard heavy footsteps approaching, which could only be his father. Cornelius Taylor was an imposing man, tall, like his sons, at six feet three with a shock of silver hair usually covered by a Stetson.

"Ah, just the son I wanted to see," his dad said, his large frame filling the doorway. "I have a surprise for you. Just turn around and take a look out the window and tell me what you think."

Probably a new horse, Brandon thought as he raised an eyebrow at his dad. Brandon's true passion on the ranch was the horses, but with a foreman, stable manager and many cowboys and cowgirls, the horses were covered. Brandon was a numbers guy, and Taylor Beef was about cattle, so his area of expertise had focused on that.

Brandon wheeled his chair around and looked out past the wide front porch to the vast property, the gorgeous view of land and trees and sky. He noticed a woman, a twentysomething brunette in a tight white dress and high heels, holding some kind of tablet and looking around. He had no idea who she was.

"She's single," his dad said. "Comes from a great family. Know the Farringtons? Relatively new to Bronco Heights. Bought the Double G."

Brandon turned to his father. "And you're telling me this because…?"

Cornelius Taylor walked over to the window. "Because two birds, my son. Two birds."

Birds? What?

"Leila's an award-winning architect," Cornelius added. "I've hired her to scope out a good section of our land for a prime location for the house she'll design—for you and your future family. Who knows? Maybe you two will fall madly in love like some Christmas TV movie." He chuckled. "You get your wife and your house in one."

Brandon was *not* chuckling. In fact, he was frowning so hard his face was beginning to ache.

"There's a lot to cover in what you just said, Dad. But let's start with the house that I'm not interested in."

"Oh please," Cornelius said dismissively in a booming voice, waving his hand at Brandon. "Of course you need a grand house of your own. You're thirty-four. And when you find yourself a wife, you'll have your dream home waiting for you. Win-win. Let's go chat with Leila, shall we? Did I mention she was on the team of architects who designed BH247, that exclusive apartment complex right in town?"

Cornelius turned and headed for the door. Brandon stayed right where he was.

His dad stopped in the doorway. "Well, come on. You can talk about what style you're looking for. Log mansion? Luxe farmhouse? Of course we'll make sure the home is situated near this house so you and the family can easily come over for Sunday dinners."

It was that last part that had Brandon changing his tone. His dad was a control freak, but at heart, the man just wanted his family around the big table for pot roast. Brandon's sister had told him that, when she got really mad at their dad, she'd think of their mother, Cornelius's first wife, walking out on him, on her family, leaving him with confused young kids. Cornelius had been a workaholic, but he'd been there for his children in important ways back then. Daphne had said she knew it wasn't an excuse for their dad's controlling behavior, but it helped her understand him a bit better and be less hard on herself for not hating him for how he'd treated her since she'd moved out to start Happy Hearts.

Brandon got it. He really did. But he thought his father had gone too far with Daphne. And Cornelius was going too far now. Overstepping was the man's middle name.

"Dad, I know you mean well, but you're going to have to send Ms. Farrington on her way. I'm not in the market for a house. Or a wife. End of conversation."

Cornelius scowled. "I'll tell you what your problem is, Brandon."

Second time in a week that someone had said that to him.

"You're being offered a mansion on the property and you're turning it down," his father said. "You're your own worst enemy."

"I like my life the way it is," Brandon said. His father's only reason for building him a home on the ranch was to keep him on the ranch. That wasn't in doubt.

His father shook his head and raised his pointer finger to make another accusatory pronouncement, but he rolled his eyes and left, shaking his head.

Brandon turned toward the window and watched

his father walk up to the architect and throw up his hands. Then he heard his dad calling out, "Hey, Dirk," and saw his brother getting out of his pickup. The twins—sons from his second marriage—hadn't grown up on the ranch and didn't live here now, but Cornelius had always told them they were welcome anytime. Both liked to ride and often made use of the stables.

Run, Dirk, run, Brandon said to himself, shaking his own head. But his younger brother was trapped, and now the three of them were getting into the brunette's Range Rover and off to scout house locations. Poor Dirk probably didn't know what had hit him. Brandon had no doubt Dirk would warn Dustin to make himself scarce in the days ahead.

Brandon spun himself back around and put his feet up on the desk, next to the work he was supposed to be doing. At least he wasn't in a hot fury.

A few months ago, this kind of controlling stunt from his dad would have had Brandon all pissed off, especially because of the way Cornelius was keeping up his pointless cold war with Daphne, who'd had the gall to want her own life. His conversation with his dad would have ended quickly in raised voices and a slammed door. Now, thanks to his sister's empathy, Brandon had been focusing on trying to understand his father more, even if he didn't like it. Cornelius Taylor didn't want to lose any of his children, plain and simple. He wanted them right there in the main house, which was why he'd built addition after addition, usually with each of his marriages, to make the wings bigger and bigger. He still referred to the wing where Brandon's suite was located as the "kids' wing." Brandon could go weeks in the kids' wing without hearing another suite door open. That was how huge it was.

Brandon fully believed that his father was happy about Jordan's marriage, but he also had no doubt Cornelius was hatching plans to build Jordan and Camilla a villa on the property. Luckily, the two were on their honeymoon for a couple of weeks and didn't have to deal with Cornelius. But with Daphne having left the nest, Cornelius Taylor was digging his hooks into his second born—Brandon—who'd always been something of a wild card that couldn't be labeled or boxed. His father had a problem with that.

Cassidy Ware's lovely face and big hazel eyes floated into his mind, and what a lovely distraction it was. Perhaps he'd head over to Bronco Java and Juice for a strawberry-banana smoothie just to see Cassidy, to say hello. He could say something to let her know he hadn't just disappeared on her, that he knew she'd never take him up on his casual sex offer and he wanted to give them both some time to put the past to rest—again.

But just as he grabbed his jacket, he started thinking. And thinking. And thinking some more. He'd see Cassidy and want to kiss her. He'd ask her out on a proper date and maybe she'd say yes. Then suddenly they'd be dating. Seeing each other. She'd want more than he could give, and they'd be at each other's throats.

A montage of the romances that had almost undone him went barreling through his head. He had a thing for Cassidy and, if he gave in to it, he'd no doubt be adding her to his record of relationships that had come to a bruising end for whatever reason. Stick to the usual, he told himself. Flings and the short-term.

He threw his jacket on the love seat, sat back down and picked up the sheet of sales projections, but every time he tried to focus on the graphs, all he saw was Cassidy's beautiful face.

Chapter Three

Two weeks later

At two thirty, closing time for a café that opened at 7:00 a.m., Cassidy turned over the Open sign on the front door of Bronco Java and Juice and very slowly walked back behind the counter, her eyes on her purse. The red-leather bag with its long beaded strap was on its usual hook beside the bookcase containing her binders of recipes and special mugs and beautiful glasses she'd collected over the years. She stared at the purse, which contained something so scary she was afraid to step too close.

A pregnancy test.

It had barely been three weeks since the wedding where she and Brandon Taylor had made love in a hay-strewed stall in the stables. She tried to think of the exact date of her last period, but her head was a jumble. She only knew she should have gotten it by now. If she *was* pregnant, she'd conceived the night of the wedding.

Come on. She wasn't pregnant. First of all, she and Brandon had used a condom.

But her formerly very regular period *always* announced itself with the usual symptoms. When she'd had those for days without the actual period, she'd stopped in her tracks in the middle of the sidewalk, wondering if her strange cravings lately for a loaded baked potato with sour cream and bacon crumbles was another sign.

For peace of mind, so she could focus on her constant special orders for birthday cakes and wedding cakes—thank you Sanchez-Taylor wedding— she'd stopped into the drugstore on her break. She'd bought a test when the aisles were clear and no one was behind the counter but the kind pharmacist, who'd long been a keeper of secrets in town. What that man knew could fill a very juicy tell-all about the citizens of Bronco Heights.

Could she actually be pregnant? Barely a few weeks along? With Brandon Taylor's baby? She'd never gotten back to him on his proposal for a no-strings affair. And he hadn't followed up, which told her he hadn't been all that serious about even the most casual of relationships. A moment had presented itself in the stables and they'd both been in. Now they were both out. Fine.

Except it wasn't fine and hadn't been way before she'd even thought she might be pregnant. During the past few weeks, she'd tried to force away her traitorous feelings every time one conked her over the head or grabbed at her heart. Her feelings for Brandon Taylor had come rushing back the night of the wedding. She'd worked hard to put those feelings in their place. *You can't always get what you want and you have to deal with it.*

She thought a slightly bruised heart was all she had to contend with.

Cassidy slowly walked to her purse and dug inside for the box, then went into the employee restroom. Heart thumping, she read the instructions enclosed with the test. *"Wait two full minutes. If an orange check mark appears in the small window, you are pregnant..."*

She was sure there would be no orange check mark as she carefully followed the instructions and noted the exact time, to the second, that she placed the stick onto the sink counter. She bit her lip and paced the small bathroom without darting a single glance at the test.

You're not pregnant, she told herself. *You're just taking the test to rule it out. After this, you'll wash your hands of Brandon Taylor and how he almost scared you half to death.*

Imagine if she were pregnant with his baby? She shook her head. The man couldn't even commit to his own proposal for a no-strings fling! She let out a snort but then immediately wanted to cry.

She stared hard at the second hand of her watch. Ten, nine, eight, seven, six, five, four, three, two… one.

Cassidy swallowed. She squeezed her eyes shut and then opened them and grabbed the stick.

Bright orange check mark.

She gasped and staggered backward, grabbing the edge of the sink to steady herself.

What?

She stood staring at the check mark, one hand going instinctively to her belly.

Pregnant.

But they'd used a condom. Could it have broken?

She closed her eyes, her heart thumping, her head feeling like it was stuffed with hay.

Maybe because she was in shock, she grabbed her phone and found the "hi" text Brandon had sent her at the wedding. At least she had his number and didn't have to track him down at the ranch. She texted him.

I'm at Java and Juice. Can you come here now? Very important.

He texted back within five seconds, which she found sort of comforting.

Sure thing. Be right there.

Well, at least he responded fast—not only to her text, but to the word *important.* He'd get here soon, she'd tell him, and they could be in shock together.

She stood in front of the mirror, looking for differences. She had to look different if she were pregnant. Something telling in the eyes. But she looked just the same as she had this morning.

Cassidy paced with the stick of the pregnancy test, eyeing the orange check mark. Pregnant, pregnant, pregnant.

Maybe she should have *first* called a trusted friend, like Callie. Talked it out and come to some kind of understanding about the different possible scenarios. But there was only one scenario she could think of right now. Having this baby on her own because Brandon Taylor was going to move to Alaska when he found out.

Cassidy Ware, a single mother. Like her mother before her.

Whatever you do, Cassidy, don't get yourself pregnant by some guy, her late mother had said quite a few times over the years. *Yeah, a baby is a beautiful and precious thing, but the reality of raising a child alone—emotionally, physically, finan-*

cially and spiritually—is harder than most people can imagine. Be smart with yourself, girl.

Tears stung Cassidy's eyes and she blinked them away. What she would give to have her mother back right now. Her mother's mother had been gone when Cassidy wasn't even two years old, and there had been very little in the way of a support system for her mom.

"Hello?" a deep male voice called out from the front of the shop. "Cass?"

He was as good as his word. Not ten minutes had elapsed since they'd texted.

"Cass?" he called again.

The sound of his voice sent a surge of protectiveness through her and she put her right hand on her belly.

No matter what, she said to her stomach. *I will do right by you. That's a promise.*

She wasn't sure she meant to, but she came out of the bathroom with the stick in her hand. Brandon was standing in front of the counter, concern on his face.

She stared at him, then looked at the stick.

He gaze went right to it, his dark eyes widening.

"What's that?" he asked, staring from it to her and back to the stick. He stepped closer, staring harder.

"According to this, I'm pregnant."

His head leaned slightly forward and now his expression held confusion and shock. "Pregnant?"

"Pregnant," she repeated.

He didn't say anything for a few moments. "And how do you feel about this?"

The question surprised her. She'd expected him to ask why she was telling him this. Then demand a paternity test. Then head for Alaska.

How do I feel about this? she asked herself. *I don't know. I don't know. I don't know.* She hadn't had time to even think about it. "I don't know yet. I'm processing. I'm still in shock, which is probably why I called you instead of a close girlfriend to help me get my head around it."

The one thing she did know? She was going to have a baby. A sudden elation whirled through her, but in seconds it was gone, replaced by fear.

She needed a little time to get her bearings here. "Coffee?" she asked, her throat dry. "Smoothie?" She pointed at the colorful chalkboard listing the offerings. "We can sit down and talk. But for a few minutes, our most pressing issue can be what we're in the mood for. I think I'll have the Berry Explosion smoothie."

He looked at her, head slightly tilted, expression unreadable. "Actually, I would love a strawberry-banana smoothie. I've kind of been avoiding this place ever since you opened it despite my love of juices. And coffee. And pastries."

She smiled. "Coming right up. And since the blender is so loud, we can be spared having to make small talk." She grabbed her big knife and headed for the baskets of fruit and the chopping board.

He looked relieved and dropped into a chair at a table for two, then immediately sprang up. "Can I help? Should you be up and about?"

She stared at him, not expecting that, either. Her guard was way up with Brandon Taylor, but every now and then, he'd make it dip a bit. She had to be on guard against that. "Pregnant women can lift bananas. No worries."

He nodded a few times, then sat back down. Every time she looked over at him, he was looking at her.

I am pregnant with your child. The words kept echoing in her head. How was this her reality? A literal roll in the hay, a half hour after fifteen years of avoidance, and she was pregnant. With Brandon's baby.

She gave her head a little shake, snapped lids on their cups and brought over a berry smoothie for herself and his strawberry banana. She sat across from him. He pulled out his wallet, and she covered his hand with hers. "On the house."

"Thanks," he said, putting his wallet away. He very slowly unwrapped his straw and then slid it into the lid, finally taking a long sip. "Delicious.

And fortifying. I actually don't feel like I might fall over anymore."

"Is that how *you* feel about it?" she asked.

He took another sip of his drink. "The news is a shock, I won't lie. But everything's going to be fine. We'll get married."

She froze. "Married?"

"Married. We're having a baby, Cassidy. So, yes, let's get married."

"Just like that, you're proposing marriage?" She reached up and put the back of her hand to his forehead. Not hot at all. "Brandon, you didn't even follow through on proposing a no-strings affair."

"Because you deserve more than that, Cassidy."

"You mean because you don't want to deal with me demanding more from you," she countered. She had this guy's number. Please.

"Maybe both. But all that is moot now. We're having a baby. So let's get married for the baby's sake."

Part of her wanted to cry. The other part was drawn to the practicality of it. But her answer was no.

"Never in a million years would I marry without love being the driving force," she said.

"Marriage can be about partnership. It can be about us as a team, taking care of our child."

"Ah, so how would that work? You would have 'married hours' where you would dote on your child and make dinner for the family and then in your free time you'd sleep with other women as if you weren't married?"

"Of course not!" he said. Loudly. "Sorry. If we marry, we're married. I'm not going to date, Cassidy. Jeez."

"So you'd be all-in for a partnership to raise our baby. Interesting. I have to say, you've surprised me. I didn't think you'd take the news well at all, and here you are, preparing to forsake all others. But the wedding vows include loving your spouse. You can't pick and choose the parts of the vows you'll honor."

"We can do whatever we want, Cassidy."

She shook her head. "Some things are nonnegotiable to me. I won't marry a man who doesn't love me. You don't believe in love, so you don't seem to need it. I get it. But my answer is no."

He reached for her hand. "Well, I'm here for you, Cassidy. One hundred percent. Anything you need, say the word. I'm going to be someone's father— and I'm going to take that very seriously."

Tears stung her eyes and she looked down at her berry smoothie. Her father hadn't felt that way. But her baby's father did. Her hand went to her belly and she wanted to whisper, *Hear that, boo?*

"I'm going to be someone's father," he repeated, shaking his head. "Wow."

She smiled for the first time since seeing the

orange check mark. "I'm going to be someone's mother."

He leaned over and pulled her into a hug, and she went willingly into his arms, all her fear and worry disappearing as he tightened his hold on her. The moment he let go, all the scary emotions were back.

That made her even more unsettled. She seemed to *need* Brandon. His steady strength in the face of shocking news, his declaration to be there for both her and their baby, the comfort of his arms around her.

And because he was being so damned wonderful, she'd start relying on him.

A knock sounded at the door and a group of teens appeared, pointing at the Closed sign. "Sorry, we're closed," she called out and the group left.

"I forgot to lock up," she said.

"Why don't we go somewhere more private to talk?" he suggested. "Where do you live, anyway?"

"There are two apartments upstairs. I'm on the top floor. We can talk there. I just need to clean up."

"I'll help," he said, standing and rolling up his sleeves as he headed behind the counter.

Who are you and what have you done with the real Brandon Taylor? she wanted to say. *The arrogant rich boy who grew up with a silver spoon and gets whatever he wants because of his looks and family name.* But she realized she didn't really know Brandon at all and hadn't in fifteen years.

She was beginning to like this Brandon a little too much.

"Well, you'll have to move," Brandon said as he surveyed the tiny space that Cassidy called home. "This place is too small for one person, forget adding a baby."

He'd estimate the apartment was seven hundred square feet, if that. There was a galley kitchen that two people couldn't pass each other in, a small living room, a bedroom, a small spare room without a closet and a bathroom with a very old and tired tiled floor. The place was functional, but that was about it. No charm, no character—and not enough room for a child.

Cassidy lifted her chin. "I happen to like my apartment. It's plenty big enough for me, and a baby barely takes up any room. I'll just move my desk from the spare room to my bedroom or the living room and set up the baby's things to make a nursery."

He poked his head into the minuscule spare room, which currently held a narrow desk and chair. "How is a crib going to fit in here?"

She came up behind him and peered in. For a second, he was distracted by the scent of her perfume, something light and flowery. "I only need a bassinet to start. They're pretty small—like the baby that will sleep inside."

What else did babies need? He wasn't sure. Did he even know anyone with a baby? He tried to picture a furnished nursery.

He closed his eyes for a moment, trying to remember being very young and his dad telling him, Jordan and Daphne that he was on the way back to the hospital to bring home their stepmother, Tania, and their new twin baby brothers, Dirk and Dustin. When they'd arrived, Brandon, Jordan and Daphne had followed their dad and Tania into the enormous nursery that had two of everything. Brandon tried to picture what had been in that room.

He'd never forget the cribs—sleigh-style polished wood stenciled with the twins' names, each with a Taylor Beef cattle logo beside it. There were a few huge stuffed animals, including a giraffe whose head was practically at the ceiling. Two plush blue-and-white rocking chairs.

"Ah—you'll need a rocking chair," he said. "No way will a rocking chair fit in here."

"I'm not sure I need a rocking chair at all," she countered. "The sofa will suffice. Or I can just rock the baby as I stand."

He looked from the room to Cassidy. "You'll need a dresser. A dresser won't fit in here. And what about a bookshelf to hold the baby's books?"

"Brandon, I'm not even one month along. The baby's not reading yet."

"I like to be prepared."

"Spoken like a man who's never had to make do." She crossed her arms over her chest, chin lifted again.

He tilted his head. "Cassidy, you don't *have* to make do. You can move right into one of the furnished guesthouses on the Taylor Ranch. I'll have everything you need for you and the baby delivered immediately."

She stepped back and shoved her hands in the pockets of her white jeans. "Brandon, that's very generous of you and all, but I'm fine right here."

"Are you?" he asked, eyeing the place. The wood floors were scuffed and the apartment looked tired and old. Cassidy had done what she could—there was a plush sofa and an area rug and some framed vintage posters. But still. "I mean, when you're nine months along and can't turn around in that narrow kitchen…"

"I've been living here for five years," she said, crossing her arms over her chest again. "This is home. Sorry it's not good enough for a Taylor." She turned away, and he immediately felt like a heel.

"Cass, I'm sorry. I don't mean to pick apart your home. But right now, I'm looking at it from a different perspective—the home of the mother of my baby. I just want you to have everything. I want our baby to have everything."

She turned back to him, her expression softening—for just a moment. "Well, I do appreciate that. I mean, it's very nice that you feel that way. But our baby doesn't need *everything*."

"Were you always so stubborn?" he asked.

"Were you always so controlling?" she countered.

Knife to the heart. He could feel his frown deepening. Call him what you want, but never call him controlling, like his father. That was going too far.

"I see I hit a nerve," she said.

Yeah, you did, he wanted to say. But he was too stung and proud for that. Controlling. Him? How was wanting the best for her and their baby being controlling? Brandon was nothing like Cornelius Taylor.

He moved into the living room, shaking off the unsettling comparison. "I think we should make a list of what we'll need for the baby. If you insist on staying here, we'll need two of everything since he or she will have two homes."

Now she was frowning. "Wait a minute. Two homes?"

"You said no to marrying me, so yes, two homes. Yours and mine. I figure we'll split the week. Anyway, I'm getting ahead of myself. We won't need anything for quite a while."

"Way ahead of yourself," she agreed with a nod.

"Don't mind me, Cassidy. I think I'm just trying to wrap my mind around this as we go. Maybe it just hasn't been enough time for me to process it, so I'm throwing everything out there, trying to understand what needs to be done."

"Maybe when it does sink in, the reality of it, you won't even want to be involved," she said.

He stared at her—hard. "Not going to happen. I told you, I take this responsibility very seriously."

She stared back harder, but now there was something he couldn't quite name in her expression, in her eyes. She seemed to be trying to figure him out.

"Look, I found out I was pregnant an hour ago and four seconds later, I called you. We both need to process." She let out a yawn. "I definitely need a nap. Could be a side effect of pregnancy, but I was up till the wee hours doing a couple of test recipes for birthday cakes. Thanks to your brother's wedding, my side business is picking up serious steam."

"Side business?"

"Specialty cakes," she said. "Birthday parties, weddings. I did a seven-year-old's birthday cake for a prominent Bronco Height's family. They wanted seven layers, one for each year, each layer with a different filling—and the cake in the shape of a race car. When they said they needed it in two days and I had to turn it down, which killed me, they offered me *three hundred dollars* to do it. Three hundred dollars! Can you believe that?"

"Actually, yes. My father does stuff like that all time. 'I want it now and I'll pay for it.' That's Cornelius Taylor's motto."

"Is it yours?" she asked.

"No! Of course not. Well, I mean, if there's something important I must have, of course I'm willing to pay to make it happen."

She smiled. "I see."

He did not like the direction this conversation was going. He was nothing like his father.

"Tell me more about your side business," he suggested as she dropped down on the sofa, curling her legs up to her side.

He remembered coming into the stables the night of Jordan's wedding and seeing those legs. The legs that had started it all.

"Well, I'm trying to think of a way to put the two together," she explained. "The cake business with expanding Bronco Java and Juice. Or maybe it's two separate entities. I'm not sure yet."

"Or you could move into a bigger shop with a baker's kitchen. You already sell baked goods, so that would be a natural expansion. You've already built a great reputation and a name for yourself in both areas."

She smiled, but then it faded. "A bigger location will mean a lot more seven-layer birthday cakes. I do have two wedding cake orders that'll help that dream along."

"And I can help," he said. "We can start scouting bigger locations in the morning."

The legs unfurled and she straightened, one eyebrow raised. "Because I'm having your baby?"

"Well, yes. I'm here to help."

The legs curled back underneath her. "Brandon, I appreciate that you're generous. But I've been on my own a long time and I can take care of myself. I can make my own dreams come true."

Ah, he'd offended her at her core, but he hadn't meant to. He sat beside her, took her hands and held them. "I admire you, Cassidy. I might think you're crazy and stubborn, but I admire your independence. You're your own woman."

"I am," she said, then yawned again. She leaned back a bit so he had to let go of her hand, and she pulled the fleece throw over her and laid her head on the armrest. "I'm so sleepy."

"I'll let you get some rest." He smoothed the top of the throw and reached over to kiss her cheek.

"You're different than I thought," she whispered.

"What do you mean?" he asked, not sure he wanted her to answer that.

But she was already asleep.

Chapter Four

After leaving Cassidy's apartment—reluctantly, since he'd just wanted to sit there as she napped and let the news permeate his very thick skull—Brandon found himself driving aimlessly around town. Now that he was alone, stone-cold fear skittered up his spine and goose bumps broke out on his arms. He was going to be a dad? Someone's father? Him? Brandon was a serious enough guy, was responsible for millions of dollars at Taylor Beef, but the concept of being a helpless, dependent little being's father was scarier than it had first seemed when he was still with Cassidy. Maybe because he wasn't physically alone in the parenthood; Cassidy was the other half of that equation. But now, alone in his silver truck, he'd never felt so unsure of himself.

I need info, he thought. Information and facts. He didn't feel like going back to the ranch and using his computer because if he ran into his father, Brandon might spontaneously combust. The words *I am not like Dad* echoed through his head. Not that Cornelius didn't have his good points. But he was a know-it-all about everything, including his children's lives, and he added conflict by just being himself. Brandon did not want to be that kind of father.

But that was the question. Could a man be what his child needed instead of the fully formed person he already was? Could Brandon put his child's heart, mind and soul first? He had no idea how that worked. He'd always lived by the adages "trust your instincts" and "go with your gut." But what if his instincts were way off when it came to child-rearing? What if he'd be a terrible father? He didn't know anything about babies or children. He was about to pull over and type *How to be a Good Dad* into his phone's search engine, but who could read that tiny type?

Ah—he knew where he needed to go. A destination that would give him a good half hour to drive with purpose and end up exactly where he needed to be—in a bookstore.

He didn't bother blasting music on the way to Lewistown; he let himself sit with the startling revelation that he, Brandon Taylor, was going to be a father in eight months. That he shared this enormous responsibility with Cassidy Ware, a woman he'd had very little contact with since high school. *You'll study up, you'll be on surer footing*, he told himself as he arrived in Lewistown, a much bigger town than Bronco.

He found a bookstore and headed in, relieved that parenthood had its own section and he didn't have to ask for help. *Um, hi, do you have a book about babies for the very clueless?* He plucked out titles that sounded helpful, then put most back after flipping through them. Some had so much information jammed into the pages, including sidebar lists and illustrations that Brandon's head had started to spin. Others seemed to be written in a baby jargon he couldn't decipher. Then he found exactly what he looking for: *Baby 101 for the First-Time Father: Navigating the Unknown of a Pregnant Partner and Baby's First Year.*

He'd breathed a sigh of relief, bought two copies in case he accidentally left one somewhere, and sat in his truck in the parking space, reading. *"'You've got nine months till the baby is a living, breathing, crying, pooping part of your life. But your pregnant partner is the one carrying the baby. Check out the chart on pages 21–22 for a fetus's week-by-*

*week development and you'll have a better under-
standing of just what's going on in that growing
belly. Pregnancy is exhausting and exhilarating.
Be there for your partner...'"*

Yes, that was it. He couldn't do anything for the
baby yet; he or she wouldn't be here for months.
But he could be there for Cassidy, as he'd told her
he would be. He pulled out his phone and texted
her.

Have any cravings? I'm in Lewistown and parked
right in front of a gourmet takeout. Want some
pickles? Their menu board lists some great-
sounding soups.

She texted back immediately.

I was asleep till the phone chime from your text
woke me.

She added an emoji of a smiley face yawning.

He winced. A being-there-for-her fail. Do not
wake up the exhausted pregnant woman!

He waited a beat for her to text what food she
wanted since she was now awake, but five minutes
later, he was still waiting. "Guess she fell back to
sleep," he said to his phone.

He let the window down, the perfect midsixties
breeziness and bright September sunshine a balm.

He glanced at the book he'd set on the passenger seat. Suddenly *he* was exhausted.

What he needed was to talk to someone, someone he could trust, share this with and get some guidance from a person who actually knew him.

His sister.

Thirty minutes later he was back in Bronco, pulling into the Happy Hearts Animal Sanctuary. Happy Hearts was a registered charity animal rescue that helped farm and companion animals through rescue, adoption and education. Potbellied pigs, sheep, dogs and cats, and lots of farm animals called the place home. He texted Daphne to see if she was free to talk for a minute. She texted back that she was in the cat barn, that it was feeding time and he was just in time to help.

That was how he found himself setting down bowls of wet cat food and kibble on little mats against the walls of the adoption barn. One slinky black cat was more interested in sniffing his shoe than the food. He kneeled to give the cat a scratch on her back. She eyed him and then padded over to a bowl.

His sister, in her usual jeans and Happy Hearts long-sleeved T-shirt, her long strawberry-blond hair in a ponytail, tossed him a smile and then surveyed the room. She jotted down notes about who wasn't eating and which cats still needed their special diet, then looked at him. "Can we talk and work at the same time?" she asked. "I can hand out the bland diets while you collect kitty blankies for a load of laundry."

"Absolutely," he said, grabbing a basket in the corner, surprised when a striped gray cat jumped out and gave him a dirty look before curling up on a hay bale.

Daphne laughed. "You never know where you'll find a furry creature around here."

He started collecting the small blankets and stuffing them in the basket. Daphne sure worked hard. She had volunteers to help, but the cat barn alone was a ton of work. Then there was the dog section, and the farm animals, and who knew what else was living out its best life at Happy Hearts Animal Sanctuary, in peace and harmony. He was pretty sure there was even a very old reindeer.

"I have news," he said. "But I have to swear you to secrecy, Daphne. I need your solemn oath. Not a word to anyone."

Her mouth dropped open. "Jessica's pregnant?"

He tilted his head. Jessica? His father's third wife was not pregnant. At least, Brandon didn't think so. Then again, she was considerably younger than their dad, so anything was possible.

"Not Jessica. Cassidy Ware."

"Cassidy from Java and Juice?" Daphne asked, checking off cat names on her tablet. "What does that have to do with y—" Before she could even finish the word *you*, his sister's eyes widened. "Oh my gosh. Brandon, are you saying that you're going to make Dad a grandfather before any of us? Are you kidding me?"

"I just found out a little while ago. I'm going to be a father."

Daphne was very slowly shaking her head. "Wow. Wow!"

"I know. I don't think it's sunk in yet. Because I'm not freaking out. I mean I am, but not to the extent you'd expect."

"Interesting," she said, and he was aware that she was studying him. "And I didn't even know you and Cassidy were a couple. How long have you been together?"

When you shared one thing you might as well let it all out, he reasoned. He explained about Jordan's wedding. The stables. The champagne. Yada yada yada. Cassidy was pregnant.

Daphne was slowly shaking her head again, her blue eyes gleaming. "Wow. Wow!"

"I know," he said.

"So...since you're not even *dating*, what's the plan?"

"I immediately suggested we get married. She said no. She doesn't want to marry solely for the baby's sake. She said the man she marries has to love her."

"I'm with her," Daphne said. "No offense."

"Offense taken," he said, staring at his sibling. "What about a smooth-running partnership based on respect, shared parenthood, friendship and responsibility? That's a marriage that'll last, Daph."

She glanced at her twinkling engagement ring, then at him. "Marriages start with love. Everyone goes into it expecting the best."

"How can you be so optimistic given who our parents are?" he asked.

"I'm not saying love isn't kind of scary. Just that it's worth it. I can't wait to marry Evan next month. We're going to grow old and gray together—I have no doubt about it."

Scary? Brandon wasn't *scared* of love. He'd tried, hadn't he? Three serious relationships that had all ended miserably. If anything, thousand-year-old Winona Cobbs had been right to say he didn't know *how* to love. Anymore, that was. But he fully intended to stay rusty in that department.

Except when it came to his baby. Surely that would come naturally. Right? He needed to read more of that book. There was probably a chapter or five all about that.

He felt his shoulders slump. "Doesn't our family history make you…uneasy about it all?"

She surveyed the cats eating and checked off more boxes on her tablet, then turned it off and looked at him. "I'm not Mom. Or Dad. I make my own choices, blaze my own path."

As another black cat wound between his legs, he nodded. "That you do, Daphne Taylor." He kneeled down, setting the basket on the floor, and gave the cat a scratch on the head. He was done talking about this. Yes, he'd brought it up. He'd made a special trip over here. But he didn't feel any more in control of his own life. Control. There was that word again. Ha—he could hardly be *controlling* if he didn't even feel in control. Right?

A change of subject was definitely in order. "How do you not keep all these majestic creatures?" he asked, admiring the sleek cat.

Daphne smiled. "They have fun here. And I know they'll all find loving homes soon. They always do. Even the prickly ones who hide when a potential adopter comes in."

He gave the cat another scratch and stood. "I have this overwhelming urge to take care of Cassidy," he said out of the clear blue.

"Well, given your role in the big news, I'm glad to hear that, Brandon."

His role was father. Father. Daddy. He accepted the responsibility—absolutely. But the word itself still felt so strange applied to him. When would it feel more real? When would he be more comfortable?

"I just want to make everything easy for her," he said, his gaze on an orange tabby playing with a piece of hay. "She's pushing back. Isn't that nuts? I can give her anything she wants or needs. She can have all the creature comforts and yet she insists on staying in her tiny apartment above the shop."

Daphne smiled. "She's independent. She's been on her own since her mom died, has her own business." She scooped up the basket. She studied him for a moment and then nodded, which meant she was about to lay some of her wisdom on him. He sorely needed it. "If you want a way in, find out what she really needs, Brandon. That's how you make yourself indispensable to someone used to handling things herself."

"What she needs? But she doesn't seem to need *anything*."

"We all need something. Even you. Find out what that is for Cassidy. Maybe you can't provide it."

"With my bank accounts? Of course I can."

Daphne shook her head. "No, Brandon. I'm talking about the intangible."

He threw up his hands, and Daphne grinned.

"Get to know her," she added. "Start there. How about that?"

Get to know her. Yes, of course. He really didn't know Cassidy very well, what made her tick, what she hated and loved.

What she *needed*.

It hit him like a lightning bolt. Suddenly he understood. What Cassidy needed had nothing to do with money or diapers or cribs. He had no idea what it was, but he could find out. Then he could really be there for her.

"What would I do without you, Daph?" Brandon asked, bending to give his sister a kiss on the cheek. He took the laundry basket from her. "I'll pop this in on my way out. I have to learn how to do laundry sometime if I'm going to be someone's father."

Daphne gaped at him. "I think you're gonna be just fine, Brandon."

Maybe. Maybe not. Because the more he was getting used to thinking of himself as a dad, responsible for an innocent, precious child that he helped bring about, the more he wasn't all that sure.

Ever since Brandon's text had woken her from her nap on the sofa, Cassidy had been sitting with her laptop, feet up on the coffee table, a cup of herbal tea beside her knees, researching everything baby and motherhood. Including single motherhood. There were articles and blogs and book recommendations on the subject and everything she read had one thing in common: as a single mother, she would need a support system.

At first, she hadn't put herself in the single mother camp. Yes, she was single and she'd be a mother. But her baby's father was from the richest family in town, and whether she liked it or not, her baby would have everything he or she needed and then some. Cassidy might be independent and practical, but she wasn't stupid or stubborn to the point that she'd turn down the basics she couldn't afford on her own. She also had to consider that there were two parents here. She had her way and style and Brandon had his, and she needed to remember that she wasn't the queen; they were equal partners as parents.

And Brandon had said, more than once, that he was fully committed to being the baby's father. She wasn't on her own. But some of the articles she read had interviews with single mothers who talked about the loneliness of it all, not having the emotional support of someone who loved you. Someone to truly lean on.

Cassidy had always filled her time with work and her friends, and volunteering and dreaming of growing her business. But sometimes, when she'd come home after a particularly hard day, she'd wish there was someone special waiting for her. Someone to massage her aching shoulders and to tell her she'd make her dreams come true, that she had what it took. She'd been that for herself for years, sometimes feeling empowered and sometimes feeling so alone she'd tear up. Maybe she'd been rationalizing the freedom and focus that being single gave her.

All night she'd thought about Brandon's text,

asking if she'd like anything from the gourmet place, if she had a craving for something, and she'd been so surprised and touched that she'd had a runaway fantasy for a good twenty minutes—of imagining them together. Really together. Like married. With a baby.

She could have that, if she wanted. The man had proposed. She could have the ring, and the husband, and a nice house and everything her baby could possibly want, including a large extended family. Hadn't she very recently told Brandon she wasn't interested in marriage? That she didn't believe in it? She didn't know what she really felt and what she'd been rationalizing. What she did know was that with her mother and grandparents gone, and a couple of aunts and uncles scattered across the west, Cassidy was grateful that her baby would have all that family in the Taylors.

But she'd never been about pretending. She'd always been firmly rooted in reality. That was how her mother had raised her, and Cassidy appreciated it. Brandon might be kinder and more generous than she'd expected, but his proposal was…cold. What would be the point of marrying if there was no love? Love *was* the point.

Her phone pinged. A text from Brandon.

I got you some takeout from that place in Lewistown. Hungry?

Cassidy smiled and glanced at the clock. It was just after seven, and she was starving. I actually am, she texted back.

Be right there.

Fifteen minutes later, she buzzed him in and listened to his boots on the stairs up to the top floor. She stood in the doorway, ostensibly anticipating her deli feast but just as equally anticipating him.

She was just a little off-kilter emotionally speaking, so of course she wanted company. Company that was in the same position she was in: suddenly going to be a parent. She'd have to be careful not to get wrapped up in Brandon Taylor's grand gestures.

There he was, holding two big plastic bags from Grammy's Gourmet, one in each hand. For a moment, she couldn't take her eyes off him, all of him. The broad shoulders, that gorgeous face with the dark twinkling eyes. He wore a green Henley shirt and faded low-slung jeans that were so sexy she swallowed. And his cowboy boots. She found them sexy, too.

"I didn't know what your favorites were, so I got you a little of everything," he said. "Grammy said everything would keep in the fridge for four days."

"Did you actually ask her that?"

"Yes," he said.

She grinned. "You keep surprising me, Brandon."

"Oh, I'm full of surprises." He gave the bags a heft.

He came inside and headed to the kitchen, where he set the bags on the small round table. He took out so much food, she gasped. "Everything's labeled. I got you four quarts of soup—potato leek, Hungarian mushroom, butternut squash and roasted vegetable. I also got a lasagna, a shepherd's pie, a chicken potpie and two kinds of quiche. Also a cheesecake sampler. Oh, and a pound of ginger snaps. I remember when we dated a million years ago that ginger snaps were your favorite."

Cassidy felt tears well in her eyes. A half hour ago, she'd been uncomfortably aware that she wanted this kind of TLC in her life, and here was Brandon—the last person she'd expect it from—providing it. "Thank you, Brandon. Beyond thoughtful." She wanted to say more, but she was so touched, overwhelmed at his kindness, that she was a little speechless at the moment.

"So what are you in the mood for?" he asked.

She surveyed the crowded table. "Ever since you said chicken potpie, I've been craving it. I can taste the potatoes and carrots already."

"Coming right up," he said. "You go relax. Grammy gave me heating instructions for everything."

She stared at him. Was he for real or working some angle? What, though?

Stop being so cynical and expecting the worst, she told herself. *If a gorgeous, sexy man wants to take care of you for a change and heat up your chicken potpie, let him.*

She sat back on the sofa, charmed by the sounds of lids opening and utensils clanking on a plate. Twenty minutes later, he came into the living room with a tray and set it on the coffee table. He'd even included the salt and pepper shakers and a glass of ice water.

"Bon appétit," he said, sitting in the club chair adjacent to the sofa. "I snagged one of the ginger snaps for myself."

She was surprised to see he hadn't fixed himself a plate of something. "Not hungry?" she asked, the aroma of the chicken potpie making her mouth water.

He shook his head. "I ended up having a late lunch at my sister's farm. Do you know Happy Hearts?"

"Of course. Daphne's one of my best customers. Tries all my interesting vegetarian combos."

"Speaking of vegetarian," he said, "she insisted I try something called a seitan barbecue po'boy since she'd made one for herself earlier and had leftovers. It was so good, I had two of them, and I'm still stuffed. *Seitan barbecue.* We're talking wheat meat, Cassidy. It shouldn't be delicious, but it was."

Cassidy laughed. "Well, if you liked that, I make some amazing smoothies with silken tofu. You should try one sometime. Now that you don't have to avoid Java and Juice." She dug her fork into the potpie and blew on the steaming mouthful, then ate. Scrumptious. "This is so good. Thanks, Brandon. I owe you."

"So…does that mean you'll consider my proposal?" he asked.

She gaped at him. "I meant a smoothie on the house or something. Not marriage."

"I'll wear you down," he said, taking a bite of the cookie.

She froze, her fork midair. "Why do you want to? I mean, why do you want to get married? You don't believe in the institution."

"Because we have a different situation. We're not two people in lust who think we're going to last for the next sixty, seventy years. As I said, we'd be entering into a partnership based on shared commitment and responsibility to our baby. I believe in *that*."

She poked her fork into a chunk of potato. Romantic. Real romantic. Then again, that was what he was going for—the opposite of romance. "So, let me get this straight. For the baby's sake, for our partnership in raising our child, you'll give up the possibility of meeting someone and falling in love and wanting to marry that person for all the right reasons?"

"My reasons for wanting to marry you *are* right," he said. "But yes, I have no trouble kicking all that nonsense to the curb. Love doesn't last. People change. Love fades or dies."

Tears stung her eyes and she blinked them away fast. She wasn't even sure why she'd gotten so triggered by what he'd said, but she thought it was because of how completely down on love he was. He *really* didn't believe in it. And that was sad.

"Did you tell your sister that I'm pregnant?" she asked, taking another bite of the potpie even though her appetite was waning.

"I did. I hope you don't mind. I know it's your business, too, and I probably should have checked with you first. I did swear her to secrecy and Daphne can be trusted."

She nodded. "It's really early in the pregnancy, but if you want to tell your family, that's fine."

"How many people have you told?" he asked.

"None. Who would I tell?"

He stared at her. "What do you mean?"

"The first person I'd tell would be my mom, but I lost her five years ago. No dad to tell, and his family was never in my life. I do have a couple of aunts and cousins on my mom's side, but they live far away and we've never been close."

"Want some of my relatives?" he asked, his expression so soft on her that she had the urge to catapult herself into his arms for a hug. Just one hug to fortify her and she'd be okay again. "You can have my dad."

She laughed. "I once heard Cornelius Taylor give someone holy hell in the middle of downtown Bronco Heights. A man in a Range Rover wanted to make a right turn on red while an elderly woman was in the crosswalk and going too slow for the jerk. Boy, did your father let loose on him and his lack of respect. Cornelius took that lady's arm and helped her across the street, shooting daggers at the Range Rover dude."

"Really? Huh. My dad can *occasionally* surprise me. I wouldn't think he'd notice, let alone help anyone cross a street. No one would call him champion of the underdog. Particularly if the underdog is his own daughter. Do you know he's still mad at her for daring to leave home to start an animal sanctuary? 'How dare she mock the family business!' he bellows at least once a day. It's been *six* years. Get the hell over it, Dad."

"She's his only daughter," Cassidy said. "Surely he's supportive of her no matter what."

"Nope. He won't even acknowledge her. Turns and walks away anytime he sees her in town."

Cassidy gasped. "That's awful."

"That's family," he said. "The good, the bad and

the really ugly. No one can count on anything in this world. I mean, we both know that. We learned at very early ages that even your own parent can walk out on you. My mom. Your dad." He shook his head.

Cassidy put her fork down. She nodded; the long-running on-and-off ache in her chest fully in On mode. "I don't know which is worse. A dad walking away from his young child and never looking back? Or a dad who's been there the whole time but then turns his back because he doesn't like your choices—choices that not only hurt no one, particularly him, but help so many."

"Both bad," he said. He turned slightly, staring out the window where a big oak was just visible in the moonlight.

She studied him, and he seemed lost in thought. She wanted to ask what he was thinking about, to get him talking about the sore spots their conversation seemed to rub raw, but from his expression, she knew that would be a mistake.

"Well," he said, standing, "I'd better get going."

No, don't leave, she wanted to say. She longed to jump up and hug him.

"You okay, Brandon?" He was all tied up in knots over his family history—past and present. She understood, but if even Daphne, who'd experienced both a mother walking out *and* her father turning his back, could open herself up to love and believe in it, surely Brandon could.

Then again, she'd known siblings who were night-and-day different, so much so, she wouldn't have believed they'd been raised in the same home by the same parents.

"Okay as ever," he finally said, but she didn't understand what that meant.

You don't really know him anymore, she reminded herself. *Be careful. Protect your heart. This is not a man who's going to give you what you need most.*

He gave her hand a squeeze and then was gone, her apartment suddenly feeling so empty.

Their conversation had chased him out, but she wanted nothing more than to just be there with him, not talking. Just sitting, sharing the ginger snaps. Sharing understanding.

Yes, she was headed for big trouble where Brandon Taylor was concerned.

Chapter Five

Brandon switched on the lamp in his office, the only illumination in the room. He'd left Cassidy's almost an hour ago, and he was still too wound up to do anything relaxing, like watch the game he'd recorded or a movie. He could work; that might distract him from the thoughts jumping around in his head.

He stared at his computer screen. Yeah, right. He had way too much on his mind right now.

He thought he could commit to being a father, but how the hell did he know if he could? He was his mother's son. He was his father's son. And both Marge Taylor and Cornelius Taylor had let down their own children in the worst ways.

When Brandon was five, his father had basically bought off Margaret, who'd won custody of Jordan, Brandon and Daphne in the divorce. Back then, Brandon had thought that his mother seeking custody meant she'd loved them, cared about them—she'd fought to keep them. But she'd really been waiting for the payoff, for her mega-wealthy ex-husband to make her an offer that would justify her leaving her children. Millions. Not that Cornelius had paid her to leave them, exactly; the man had simply understood that money was more important to her than her own kids, and that had made her a poison in their lives. It was the poison Cornelius had found an antidote for. Brandon had had a love-hate relationship with his family's wealth ever since he'd learned the whole sordid story when he was a young teenager.

It was all so ugly that Brandon tried never to think about it. The screwed-up blood that ran through his veins scared him, though. Because it meant he couldn't entirely trust himself. He could say all he wanted that he'd be Father of the Year. But with his family's past, who the hell knew? And talking about it with Cassidy had gotten him so turned around that he'd had to get away before the walls closed in on him. He'd felt so claustrophobic in that moment. Not because her place was tiny but because of how uncomfortably personal their conversation had turned.

Cassidy Ware always got him talking. How did she do it? He'd had two missions in mind for going over to her place. One was to bring her the food, but the other was to answer the question Daphne had raised: what did Cassidy need?

Instead of finding out so that he could offer her what she needed and more easily convince her to marry him, they'd gotten off track. He did believe they should marry, for all the reasons he'd already stated. But also because he felt he could be a better father, a more present, everyday father, if the two of them were a couple, living in the same home, making decisions together. Given how easy it was for a Taylor to mess up when it came to relationships and family, Brandon wanted the setup to produce the best possible results. That meant marriage. Not him living at the Taylor Ranch and being a father half the week or checking in. He didn't want to be a part-time father. But unless Cassidy accepted his proposal, he'd have little choice.

Damn it.

He took a deep breath and tried to clear his mind by turning around in his chair and looking out the big windows onto the yard. But all he saw was Cassidy's face. Cassidy's swirly blond hair. Her hazel eyes. Her sexy body in her skinny jeans.

Her belly. That would soon swell with pregnancy. With his child.

His chest started to squeeze, and Brandon knew

he had stop thinking, had to get his head back in his everyday world and not the life-changing bombshell that had been dropped on him.

He grabbed his phone and checked his schedule; his day had gone off the rails with the news and the trip to Lewistown and then the hour he'd spent at his sister's farm. Scanning his to-do list, he saw he needed to get in touch with Geoff Burris, Bronco's most famous son, to sign on to promote Taylor Beef in a major advertising campaign. One of the most talented ropers Brandon had ever seen, Geoff was a huge celebrity on the Montana circuit. He'd just unseated the reigning champ over the Fourth of July weekend, and he was on his way to becoming a national hero. Scoring him ahead of the Mistletoe Rodeo in November would have Taylor Beef numbers skyrocketing.

Because Brandon had gone to high school with Geoff, though Geoff was a few years younger, Cornelius had given Brandon the job of wooing the guy into promoting Taylor Beef. Abernathy Meats, a major competitor, was after Geoff, too, and that made the negotiations harder than Brandon expected. The champ had already made clear through his management team that he'd listen to both family's pitches, but that he wasn't ready to make a decision. Brandon had some great ideas—from traditional to out of the box—but Geoff's team wasn't committing. Brandon needed to get the guy signed before the Abernathys did, or that family, with whom the Taylors had had a mostly friendly rivalry for generations, would rub it in their faces. Taylor Beef was number one, Abernathy Meats a close second. His dad and uncles wanted to keep it that way—or actually, widen the gap. Securing a star like Geoff Burris would do that.

He could try Geoff's cell phone right now. He'd had the number from years back when they'd been on the same sports team at Bronco High, Brandon as the captain and Geoff as a rising star. But calling after business hours to talk business could also piss the guy off, and that was the last thing Brandon wanted to do. He'd call in the morning. For now, he'd do some old-fashioned brainstorming with pen and paper to drum up a few new ideas for the potential advertising campaign. But ten minutes later, all he'd done was write Geoff Burris and Taylor Beef across a legal pad and tap the pen against all the blank space. Tap. Tap. Tap.

As if he could concentrate.

The fact that he could suddenly hear music playing wasn't helping. Was that a Blake Shelton song? Brandon got up and went to investigate, but stopped in his tracks the second he left his office. He could see his father and stepmother slow-dancing in the living room to the strains of a country ballad, Jessica's head on Cornelius's shoulder. Then she lifted her head and they were gazing into each other's eyes before Cornelius kissed her.

Brandon quickly backtracked into his office and shut the door. Whoa. *That* was unexpected. Had he ever seen his father and Jessica like that? He didn't think so. Honestly, he'd never paid much attention.

The two did seem happy. But was it a *for now* thing? Two marriages hadn't lasted. Why would the third be the charm?

Brandon switched off the lamp and left his office, heading for the grand stairs in the opposite direction of the living room. The music had stopped, and when Brandon started up the steps, he could see into the living room where his father and Jessica were in each other's arms.

Why the hell is life so confusing? he wondered as he went into his suite.

He pulled out his phone, the urge to call Cassidy so strong. He needed to fight that urge, tamp it down. It was one thing to want to make the mother of his child comfortable, to make sure she had what she wanted. It was another to *need* to hear her voice. He put his phone away, grumbling as he flopped onto his bed. He couldn't let himself get all twisted around. He was committing to *fatherhood*. He needed to focus on ensuring he'd be a great parent. That had to be his only personal mission.

He reached for the book he'd bought and flipped it open to his bookmark. He hadn't gotten far. But

he'd read long into the night, needing to fortify
himself with how to be the dad he *wanted* to be.

At 7:00 a.m., when Java and Juice opened for
the day, a group of customers waited for Cassidy
to unlock and flip the sign from Closed to Open.
The waiting group always made her heart happy.
And no surprise—they were all parents or care-
givers with babies.

Cassidy loved having the kiddo crowd in the
early mornings. She'd figured her early-morning
hours would attract tired parents who'd be happy
for somewhere to go before the rest of Bronco
Heights opened, and she'd been right. So Cassidy
had added a baby and toddler area with a playpen and foam mats and soft toys. Parents always
told her how much they appreciated being able to
set down their toddler at the little choo choo train
table while they sipped an iced drink and had a
brownie on the plush tan sofa along the wall beside it, or on the overstuffed chairs she'd picked up
from thrift stores.

When the babies and toddlers went home for
their naps, the en-route-to-work folks stopped
in for espressos and bagels, then she had coffee-
breakers and snack-needers who poured in and out
till noon when the lunch crowd started arriving.
The menu, offering everything from sandwiches
and soups to crepes and pastries, brought in a var-

ied customer base from the 7:00 a.m. to 2:30 p.m. hours.

A baby squealed as Cassidy was headed back behind the counter, and she turned to smile at the babies on laps and in the playpen, a toddler picking up one of the little colorful trains.

I'm going to be a mother, she thought, her smile turning into a grin. *Maybe not the way I'd always imagined, but that's okay. More than okay.*

She'd spent a lot of time thinking about Brandon last night, about what a surprise he'd turned out to be, including hidden depths, and she'd had to issue another warning to protect herself. She had a lot going on. Running a business required her full attention, and now she had to split that attention with everything being pregnant required—from getting used to the idea itself, to doing some research and making lists.

As Hank and Helen, a wonderful married couple in their late sixties who'd started working for Java and Juice after their retirement, were in the kitchen making the popular breakfast sandwiches and slathering various kinds of cream cheese on bagels, Cassidy took orders and made drinks. There was a good number of people waiting in line, babies and strollers inching up, and she felt her heart ping with pride. *I might not have achieved everything I intended, but this is my shop and it's paying the bills. I can take care of my baby just fine. And*

I don't have to do that from a luxe guest cabin at the Taylor Ranch.

As the morning wore on, Cassidy made smoothies and juices and coffee drinks, selected pastries from the display, handed over turkey BLTs, soups, and banana-chocolate crepes, and swiped many a credit card. She grinned when she saw her next two customers. Her friend Callie Sheldrick holding ten-month-old Maeve Abernathy. Maeve was the daughter of Tyler Abernathy, Callie's widowed boyfriend. Callie explained she had the day off from her job as an admin at Bronco's Ghost Tours so she was caring for the little one today.

"A little on-the-job training for someday," her friend whispered down to the baby in a stroller beside her. Callie's brown eyes shone with pure happiness. Cassidy could tell she adored the baby.

Speaking of… Maybe she'd share her big news with Callie. Aside from Brandon's family, Cassidy didn't want everyone to know, not this early in the pregnancy, but she'd sure like to talk over motherhood with a good friend. She glanced up at the big round clock on the wall. Ten minutes till her break.

Cassidy handed Callie her chocolate-almond smoothie, then hurried around the counter to say hi to the sweet baby when a little fist reached out and grabbed the end of her long ponytail. She swallowed her yelp. Maeve let out a huge laugh that couldn't possibly come from such a small body.

Cassidy grinned at her friend. "That's some grip!"

Callie gave the baby a tickle and she immediately let go. "Tricks of the trade. She once had my hair in a death grip and I finally learned that blowing a raspberry on her shoulder made her release and give out that great belly laugh."

Cassidy wished she were writing all this down. These were the small details she'd need to know. "I go on break in a few. I'll join you. I have news," she whispered.

"Oooh, I will be all ears," Callie said and then settled at a table near the baby section.

Cassidy made many more drinks, had to restock her cinnamon crumb cake, a big hit today, and the coconut-chocolate-chip scones, and then finally it was break time. She fixed herself a berry smoothie and headed over.

The baby was in her stroller beside Callie's seat, her blue eyes drooping. Cassidy pulled over a chair, unable to take her eyes off Maeve, her soft blond-brown wispy curls, beautiful face and pink bow lips, the tiny nose, the rise and fall of her chest as she dozed off. Cassidy was suddenly overcome with a wave of butterflies flying around her stomach. At the responsibility of raising a child. Unlike Brandon, Cassidy had no doubt of her capacity to be a good parent, but that didn't mean she wouldn't make mistakes. And the sight of baby Maeve, such a marvel of a tiny human being, made her long to be perfect, a TV mom who had all the answers.

She bit her lip, suddenly overwhelmed and unable to get any words out.

Callie peered at her. "What? What's wrong, Cass?"

"I'm pregnant," she whispered, glancing around to make sure no one was listening to their conversation.

Her friend's eyes widened. "Tell me everything."

Cassidy did. Starting with the stables, then describing the business-like marriage proposal and ending with how incredibly kind and thoughtful Brandon had been. She even told her friend about him bringing her four kinds of soup and heating up her chicken potpie.

"Wow," Callie said. "Sure sounds like he's going to be a great dad if he's that caring."

Cassidy took a sip of her smoothie to try to stop herself from what she was about to say. It didn't work. "And a man a little too easy to fall in love with."

There it was. Maybe what really had her so anxious.

"Ah, gotcha," Callie said. "I see the problem. But eight months is a long time, Cass. And perhaps just the right amount of time for a self-confirmed bachelor like Brandon to come to a few realizations."

Cassidy felt herself brighten. That was true.

Maybe Brandon did just need some time with all
these new developments. Becoming a dad and dealing with the hold his family's past had on him. Realizing that a marriage without love was cold and
empty. She certainly didn't expect him to want
to marry her because he loved her; they barely
knew each other at this point. But she *would* like
him to propose they begin a real relationship—a
good start.

"I'm just starting to get to know Brandon," Cassidy said. "And, to my big surprise, I like him. A
lot. But that might be just the situation talking,
the newness, the shock, and the reaction to how
insanely sweet Brandon is being. Aside from the
business deal of a marriage proposal."

"Well, even that was sweet," Callie said, taking
a sip of her smoothie. "He's giving up everyone
else for you and the baby. That says something."

"It really just says he doesn't care about love.
That's what he's giving up."

Callie shook her head. "Hardly, my friend. Bronco's Most Eligible Bachelor is giving up *other*
women, Cass. No dating. No sex. If he's proposing a marriage without love or romance, obviously
he knows he's saying 'see ya' to sex, too."

Now it was Cassidy's eyes that widened. "I
didn't think about it. I mean, I really didn't have
a chance to consider what his idea of partnership-

marriage would mean...how we'd operate, you know?"

"If he's giving up sex with all the hot singles in Bronco, then he either intends to have a sexual relationship with his wife or he's truly suggesting a partnership and he cares more about you and the baby than he does about his sex life."

"Huh. We already nixed a no-strings romance," Cassidy explained.

"Um, Cassidy? I'd say a legal document like a marriage license is strings aplenty."

Cassidy tilted her head. "Callie, you're blowing my mind. I can't take this all in! Don't say anything else."

Callie chuckled. "You have a lot to think about. But I suggest having a conversation with Mr. Taylor about exactly how he envisions this marriage to go. Not that you'd say yes, but you should have all the information."

It *was* a lot to think about. Cassidy sat back and sipped her berry smoothie. Jeez. Now she understood a little of how Brandon had felt last night, why he'd up and bolted. Cassidy felt like doing that right now—running out the back door to just stop and breathe for a few minutes, digest what her friend was saying. It was all too much.

Woof! Woof, woof!

Cassidy bolted up. "That might be Maggie! The

dog you said went missing from a Happy Hearts adoption event."

Before Cassidy had known about the missing Maggie—she'd sort of named the adorable stray who'd been coming around the back door at Java and Juice Scooter. At first she thought Scooter must belong to someone nearby and was allowed to roam around the back alleys. She'd put out treats and spend a little too much time talking to Scooter, sharing her hopes and dreams. Animals sure were easy to talk to.

Cassidy was hopeful that the dog would still be there when she opened the back door, but the sweet pooch was gone.

"Hopefully she'll come back," Callie said as Cassidy returned to the table. "If she does and you can leash her, call Daphne and she can come by to check to see if it's Maggie."

"I definitely will," Cassidy said.

The front door opened and a bunch of customers came in, including Tyler Abernathy, Callie's boyfriend. The tall, lean rancher took off his cowboy hat, nodded at Cassidy and then smiled at Callie. "I was missing my two sweethearts so I figured I'd come in for a coffee and get to see you both even for just a few minutes."

Tyler leaned down to give Callie a kiss, then gazed at her and his napping daughter with such love that Cassidy's heart skipped a beat.

Love. Pure love. *It might be really hard to come by, but it exists and I'm holding out for it*, Cassidy thought.

"So your mom is all set with babysitting tonight, right?" Callie asked him. She turned to Cassidy. "An old friend of mine is in a community theater production of *Romeo and Juliet*. I'm so excited about a night on the town."

Ping!

Tyler pulled out his phone. "Uh-oh," he said. "Guess who just texted me she can't babysit tonight because Dad just came down with a cold."

Cassidy looked at Maeve. *She* could watch the baby. And learn something in the process. "I'd be happy to babysit this little pumpkin."

"I really appreciate that," Tyler said, "but we need an *overnight* sitter. The play starts late and ends late and then there's a dinner and party after."

Oooh, Cassidy thought, *an overnight with a baby. Now that would provide some serious on-the-job training.* "No worries. I'll babysit at my place. Just drop off her bassinet, and whatever she might need for the night. Then just pick her up in the morning from here."

Callie slid her a happy glance that told Cassidy her friend understood why she was so eager to babysit—and overnight, at that.

Tyler looked so relieved. "You sure you don't mind? She's an easy baby, but she might wake up

once during the night. She's pretty good at soothing herself back to sleep, though."

Cassidy grinned. "I'd *love* to watch Maeve. Really, it's my pleasure."

Callie smiled and squeezed her hand. "We'll
drop her off on the way. Seven?"

"Sounds good," Cassidy said, so excited about
her evening's adventure.

As the trio left, Cassidy wondered if she should
invite Brandon over to help. So that he could get
a sneak peek at what taking care of a baby was all
about. He seemed truly committed to his role as a
father, and she doubted he was all talk; his actions
truly said otherwise. But a preview of what caring
for a baby entailed, particularly in the wee hours
of the morning, might have him changing his tune.
And if it did, she needed to know that now. That
would easily call a screeching halt to her blossom-
ing feelings for Brandon.

As if he knew she was thinking about him, her
phone pinged with a text from him.

How are you feeling today? Need anything?

The warm fuzzies enveloped her. He probably
had no idea how such a simple question, maybe just
a nicety for him, meant to her. If her mother were
still alive, she'd be calling Cassidy every hour on
the hour to check in. She'd bring tons of comfort

food, all safe for pregnancy. She'd bring her wool socks and a new cozy throw. She'd care the way mothers cared.

And here was Brandon, a man who professed that he wasn't interested in love, being very loving.

I feel great—thanks for asking. I told Callie the big news. And I'm babysitting little Maeve Abernathy tonight at my place if you want a sneak preview of what to expect. Any time after 7:00.

She waited, wondering if this would be it, when he would show his true colors, make an excuse about why he couldn't. As if he'd want to babysit with her. As if he'd want to take care of a baby any earlier than he absolutely had to. Come on, Cassidy.

I'll be there, he texted back.

She let out a wistful sigh. Of course, he would. Because that seemed to be who Brandon was. A man she could count on. Though a man she could count on to be exactly what he'd said he'd be: a committed father to their baby, a committed platonic partner to Cassidy. Nothing more.

Just remember where you stand and you'll be fine, she told herself.

Chapter Six

"You're doing *what*?" Cornelius asked, confusion-tinged anger exploding on his face.

"I'm babysitting," Brandon repeated, never so grateful to have an excuse for getting out of the fundraiser his dad was trying to get him to go to in his stead tonight. Brandon had lost count of the number of high-ticket fundraisers he'd gone to this year. Between the monkey suit and the small talk, he couldn't take another.

The two stood in the grand foyer of the ranch house, Brandon slipping on his jacket.

"Not that part!" his father bellowed. "Though why you would be babysitting is beyond me, but

I'll tell you, Brandon, you're not always easy to understand."

Brandon stared at his dad. "Then what part?"

"You're helping an *Abernathy*? Consorting with the enemy!"

Oh brother. "I don't think fifteen-pound Maeve Abernathy is any threat to us, Dad."

"Those Abernathys are living for the day they catch up to Taylor Beef in revenue," Cornelius said, waving his index finger around. "This has to be a setup. Tyler is probably going to pick your brain for how you're planning to secure Geoff Burris in our new ad campaign, then steal all the ideas and Burris himself!"

Good Lord. "There's not going to be any discussion of business. In fact, I doubt Tyler even knows I'll be helping out tonight."

Cornelius perked up at that. "Oh. Helping out who?"

"Cassidy Ware. She's the actual babysitter."

"Cassidy? That nice gal who owns Java and Juice?"

He knew the place? That was a surprise. "Yes. You've been there?" Despite his fortune, his dad wasn't one to "throw good money away" on what he could "have for free at home." Like coffee. And lunch. And would Cornelius Taylor ever drink a concoction made from silken tofu and kale? No.

Vegan nonsense, he called smoothies, even the ones made with milk.

"Jessica likes that place, so we stop in there on occasion," Cornelius said. "Last time, she had many questions about the juice blends and wasn't sure which she wanted to order, and Cassidy offered to make her as many samples as she wanted to try. Now that's good business sense. Jessica liked so many of the samples, she ordered a bunch of quart containers to bring home. Cassidy said we were the first to order by the quart. We must have dropped a hundred bucks in there that day."

Brandon almost pumped a fist in the air. *Go, Cassidy.*

"And I thought you two hated each other," his dad added. "Something about a bad romance in high school?"

"We've become...friends," Brandon said. He made a show of pulling out his phone and checking the time. "I'd better get going."

"Fine," Cornelius grumbled. "But if you see that Abernathy, you tell him nothing! Not a word to him about Taylor Beef or Burris. Nothing! Tyler will probably come out with the baby in his arms to seem all harmless and fatherly, then go in for the kill about your pitch to Burris's team."

Brandon shook his head with a smile. "Don't worry, Dad."

"Oh, I will. That's my job."

Brandon clapped his dad on the shoulder. "See you later."

Once in his truck, Brandon let out a deep breath. Talking about Cassidy with his father had felt so strange, given the big news Brandon was withholding. *Yes, Cassidy from Java and Juice—generous with samples and the mother of your soon-to-be grandchild.*

He was far from ready to share that last part.

Brandon made a brief stop in town to pick up a few things, and when he finally pulled into a spot near Cassidy's place, he saw Tyler and Callie getting into their car and driving off. *See, Dad, I told you. No worries. No point of contact made.*

He pressed the intercom for Cassidy's apartment and she buzzed him in. He took the steps two at a time, his anticipation at seeing her making him a little uncomfortable. She was waiting in her doorway when he reached the top floor. Her blond hair was in a bun, exposing the neck he'd kissed every inch of not too long ago. She wore a long-sleeved, green-and-white Bronco Java and Juice T-shirt and soft, faded jeans. He thought she was sexy in a slinky cocktail dress? Whoa.

She held the baby in her arms. The little girl had a small purple rattle in her hand. "Look who it is, Maeve! It's Brandon!"

He grinned. "Hi there, Maeve. I'm going to help babysit tonight."

Maeve stared at him and shook the rattle. "Abda!"

"Nice to meet you, too," he said. "I'm just learn-
ing how to speak Baby, so go slow, okay?"

Cassidy smiled. "I love her babbles. She's just
the cutest," she added, giving the baby a snuggle.

He followed Cassidy inside and lifted his gift
bags. "So, I brought over a couple of things."

Her hazel eyes sparkled. "Do you ever just show
up?"

"No. How could I not get a little something for
the baby?"

She laughed, shaking her head. "I wish you'd
stop being thoughtful, Brandon. You make it hard
for me to put you in a certain box."

"Right. Because labels are ever accurate. People
are never just one thing."

"Touché," she said with a nod. "He's got me
there," she added to Maeve, then sat in the living
room, the baby on her lap, Brandon beside her.

"So, for you, Miss Big Cheeks, I have this."
He pulled out the soft, floppy, stuffed bunny with
bright orange ears and a yellow body. Maeve
dropped the rattle on the floor, grabbed the bunny
and started shaking it. Its hands rattled and were
chewable, which the teething baby apparently dis-
covered because a hand went right in her mouth.

Cassidy grinned. "It's a hit."

"I did get help picking it out from the salesclerk
at the gift shop. I had no idea what to get a baby,

but she asked me the age and came back with a few suggestions." He picked up the other bag and handed it to her. "Just a little something for you."

"Brandon! You didn't have to get me anything." She peered inside and pulled out the small hardcover book. *Comforting Quotes, Wisdom, and Lullabies for the New Mother.* She touched her hand to her heart. "Darn you, there you go again. I love books like this. Thank you." She flipped through it, stopping on a page near the beginning. "'Nap when the baby naps,'" she read. "'Ignore the laundry, the dust bunnies, your to-do list, turn off your phone, and rest.' Sounds like excellent advice to me."

He nodded. "I saw it by the counter and thought you might like it."

"I do. Very much. Thank you."

"So what's on the agenda?" he asked, eyes on the baby. "Does she have a schedule? According to my fatherhood book, schedules are everything." He was only on chapter four, but he'd learned quite a bit and was looking forward to putting what he knew in practice tonight.

"You have a book on fatherhood?" she asked.

"Yup. Bought it the day I found out I was going to be a dad. I have to read every sentence very slowly since all the lingo is new. Did you know there are different kinds of cries? Pick me up *now* cry. Hungry cry. Tired cry. Bored cry. My belly hurts cry."

Cassidy laughed. "I've also been doing research and reading. Baby world is definitely its own universe. And yes, Maeve has a schedule. Tyler gave me a cheat sheet of everything to know about Maeve. When to feed her, when to put her down for the night, what to do if she cries in the middle of the night, when to expect her to wake up in the morning, how much to feed her. Everything."

Whoa. He hadn't gotten that far in the book. The subject of "sleep" alone had three chapters. "That sounds like a lot to keep track of. What is she up to now?"

"Just chillin'," Cassidy said. "She'll be ready for her bottle soon and then we'll have more playtime and then we'll put her in her crib for the night. Tyler said she tends to sleep through. Well, till five, five thirty."

"Hey, I work at a ranch. We get up with the roosters. Five is nothing to me."

"I hadn't considered that. You'll be fine with the early mornings, then. Me, too, since the shop opens at seven, and I bake fresh beforehand."

He immediately pictured himself beside her in bed, Cassidy naked and sleeping, her blond hair splayed on the pillow. He'd hear their baby cry in the middle of the night and go take care of him or her, letting Cassidy sleep. He'd follow the schedule and, when the baby was ready for a nap, he'd get back under the covers with Cassidy. No problem.

He'd heard that taking care of a baby was tough stuff, but between his fatherhood book and some practice like tonight, he'd pick it up in no time. He'd have a *schedule*. Just like he had for his workdays. And didn't babies nap all day in their cribs or strollers? Most times he noticed a baby in a stroller in town, the little one was snoozing away peacefully, not making a peep.

He liked everything about his middle-of-the-night scenario and baby-rearing with Cassidy, except getting out of their bed. Of course, there wasn't going to be a "their bed." She'd turned down the no-strings romance. She'd turned down the platonic marriage proposal. Maybe he'd broach the subject of marriage again tonight. Taking care of a baby while talking about providing a united Team Parents might sway Cassidy.

"Would you like to hold her?" she asked.

He almost jumped. Did he want to hold her? *No*, he thought. Maeve seemed pretty fragile. Droppable. Breakable. Had he ever held a baby? He couldn't remember ever doing so. Damn. A minute ago he was all "there's nothing to taking care of a baby." Now he was afraid to hold one. No one ever said he didn't talk a good game; he was kind of famous for it. But usually he came through. Now he just wanted to inch away. "Do you need a break?"

She tilted her head. "Not necessarily. I just thought you'd want to. You don't have to. But unless you've had lots of interactions with babies, you might like to see what's it all about."

"I've had zero interaction with babies," he admitted. He wasn't sure why that was so hard to say. He didn't like coming up short. But this was one area where Brandon Taylor, Executive VP, had absolutely no experience.

"See how I'm holding her?" Cassidy asked. "Supporting her against my chest with an arm around her back and one under her bottom? That's what you do. It'll be instinctive once you take her," she added. "How tightly to hold her, all that."

"Okay," he said, holding out his hands.

He didn't have his arms in the correct position, so Cassidy adjusted them and suddenly Maeve Abernathy was against his chest, holding on to her bunny and chewing away on its toe. He stared down at the top of her head in complete wonder. He had a baby in his arms!

"She barely weighs anything and yet feels so substantial." He sniffed the top of her head. "Baby shampoo. I remember when my twin brothers were babies and smelled like that." He looked down at Maeve, then over at Cassidy.

"I love that smell," she said. "I think everyone does. And you're doing great, by the way," she added with a nod. "You look like a natural."

He raised an eyebrow. "You're lying through your teeth."

"Nope," she said, shaking her head. "You really do."

Huh. That gave him a bit more confidence. Could he move and hold Maeve at the same time? He stood and walked over to the windows. That shouldn't have felt like such an accomplishment, but it absolutely did. "Look, Maeve, that's a tree. And there's a man walking a little dog. I think it's a Boston terrier." She turned her huge eyes to him and shook her bunny. "Yeah, the doggie is very cute. I agree."

"Bah!" Maeve said, waving her bunny before dropping it.

He eyed the stuffed animal on the wood floor. "Hmm, do I have the super powers of kneeling down while holding a baby and picking that up?" he asked Cassidy.

She grinned. "Slowly."

He knelt as slowly as he could, keeping a tight hold on Maeve, and reached out an arm and grabbed the stuffed animal, which Maeve batted right out his hand and back onto the floor. She then exploded into baby laughter. He picked it up again, and again she knocked it to the floor, giggling away.

"Oh, it's like that, is it?" he asked, giving her a little tickle on her belly. More baby laughter. He had no idea babies could laugh that loud.

He looked over at Cassidy, who wasn't laughing. Or smiling. "Everything okay?" he asked.

"Yeah," she said. "Everything's fine. She turned away and sat on the sofa, straightening the little pile of white burp cloths that were already perfectly stacked on the coffee table.

Hmm. Something was not fine. He walked to the couch and stood beside it, Maeve now batting his chin with the stuffed animal. He gave her another tickle and she dropped the bunny with a giggle.

"So this is how babies play games," he said. "I thought they just sat around or napped. I'm getting a first-rate education here, thanks to you," he added, giving Maeve's impossibly soft cheek a gentle caress. He sat beside Cassidy, the baby now nibbling on her fingers. "You have a lot of experience with babies? Kids of your friends? Relatives?"

"Neither," she said. "But I have done a lot of babysitting. It's how I put myself through school and got my associate's degree. Well, that and waitressing."

"Are all babies like Maeve? I like her. She has spunk."

Cassidy laughed and he was so glad to hear that sound. She'd seemed a bit down a minute ago. "There's a huge range. You've got your colicky screamers." She shivered. "Then you've got never-nappers. Then there are the easy-peasies, like Maeve seems to be."

As if on cue to take issue with that, the baby let out a cry, not a cry-cry, more like a fussy whine.

"Ah, let me check the schedule," Cassidy said. "I think it's time for her dinner and bottle." She scanned the typed, stapled pages and stopped mid-page with her fingertip. "Seven thirty, dinner. One container of mac and cheese, two peach slices and four ounces of formula in her bottle."

"Wow, she eats mac and cheese?" he asked. "I figured she'd eat jarred baby food. Sweet potato purée. Apple sauce."

"She's a few months past solids, so she can eat tiny bites of just about anything," Cassidy said. "Tyler dropped off a small container for her. He told me he makes a batch of her meals for the week and freezes them and sometimes she eats whatever he and Callie are having, just little pieces."

Brandon smiled. "Tyler sounds like a great dad. I should talk to him. Not that I'm *allowed* to talk to him." He groaned and rolled his eyes.

"Not allowed?" she asked with a raised eyebrow as she stood and headed into the kitchen.

Brandon followed. "My father thinks Tyler set up this entire babysitting scenario so that he can corner me for information about Geoff Burris. Taylor Beef and Abernathy Meats are major competitors and both want Geoff to sign on to promote the company in an ad campaign."

"Ah," she said. "Your dad doesn't really believe

Tyler set this up, does he?" She slid Maeve into the baby seat rigged to the table, then went to the refrigerator and took out a small container and a baby bottle.

"Oh, he probably does. Two plus two always equals a lot more than four with my dad. He has all sorts of equations to make facts add up the way he wants. All he needed to hear was that I was going over to your place to help babysit an Abernathy."

Cassidy smiled. "Maeve is totally innocent!"

"He figures Tyler will jump out of the wood-work at some point to get me to talk about my secret plan to sign Burris."

"Landing the biggest rodeo star in Montana would be major," she said. "*Do* you have a secret plan?"

"Well, I've tried every business tactic I've learned over the years and that didn't get me past his 'team,' so yes, I now do have a secret plan that I will put into effect tomorrow."

"Can I hear it?" she asked, pouring the contents of the container into a small pot and turning on the burner.

"Sure. It's called 'I knew you in high school.'"

Cassidy laughed. "Will that work with him? If it were me in his shoes, I would sign with Abernathy Meats just to spite you."

He grinned. "Yes, you would have. Before you

re-knew me. Admit it, now you'd sign with Taylor Beef."

"Well, I am going to have a little Taylor, so yes," she said.

His gaze went right to her belly, still completely flat. But in there was a tiny, growing mix of the two of them. He swallowed and suddenly had to sit.

He pulled out a chair and sank down on it, right next to Maeve, who was banging her bunny on the tray top of her seat. *I get you, Maeve,* he said silently to her. *You're a little frustrated, just like I am, so you're slamming your bunny. If it were okay for me to do that, I would.* She swiveled her big blue eyes to him. *Not that I don't like babies. I'm gonna have one in, what...eight months? Sometimes that sinks in and scares the bejesus out of me, Maeve. Again, no offense.*

"So we're okay?" he asked the baby.

"Ba la!" Maeve said and flung the bunny across the table.

She let out a giggle before her face crumpled and her eyes got teary. Boy, did her face go from its normal complexion to bright red.

"Just in time!" Cassidy said, bringing over a little plate of mac and cheese.

Maeve's expression changed in a snap at what was before her. Cassidy slid a baby spoon into one piece of macaroni and brought it up to the baby's lips. Maeve gobbled it up.

Looked easy enough. "I'll feed her," Brandon said. "You cooked, so I've got this."

Cassidy smiled and handed him the spoon. "I'll get her peaches cut up." She walked over to the refrigerator again, her back to him.

Again, he got the feeling that something was wrong, that *something* was bothering her. Ask? Don't ask?

"Everything okay?" came tumbling out of his mouth, even though he probably should have just let her be with whatever was going on inside her head. He didn't always want to answer that very question whenever it was asked of him. In fact, he never did. So he should extend the same courtesy to Cassidy.

She turned toward him with a tight smile. He could see something was warring within her. Her hazel eyes seemed half happy and half upset. "Of course," she said—too brightly—then got busy with a knife and the peach slices.

Brandon nodded and turned back to Maeve, feeding her another little cheesy macaroni, then another and another. She batted the next spoonful at his face, and the gooey pasta clung to his chin. "Oh, thanks, Maeve."

Cassidy laughed, so hard that he couldn't help but laugh, too. Then she stopped, kind of suddenly, and looked like she might burst into tears.

As he wiped the macaroni off his face, he

thought about his sister telling him to find out what Cassidy *needed* and that once he did, he'd become indispensable and then she'd come around to marrying him. Whatever it was that she needed, she wasn't getting it right now. That was for sure.

Something was definitely bothering Cassidy. And he was going to find out what.

Yes, something was wrong, she thought as she watched Brandon settle onto the sofa with Maeve on his lap. After he fed the baby, Cassidy had changed Maeve into her jammies, a soft cotton one-piece with blue moons and yellow stars. While she'd done that, Brandon had taken the storybook from Maeve's bag and flipped through it. Now, with Maeve reclining against him, her head in the crook of his elbow, he began reading aloud from *Doolie the Duck's Big Adventure*.

A few pages in, he noticed the baby's eyes drooping and his voice lowered, the sound almost lulling Cassidy to sleep, too. "Well, Maeve, I only got to read you four pages. Maybe next time I'll get to find out if Doolie and the beaver become buddies." He smiled, gently pushing back a baby curl from near Maeve's eye.

This. This was what was wrong.

The man was a revelation. She kept expecting him to revert to the Brandon Taylor she'd thought he was the past fifteen years. An arrogant hot-shot leaving behind the ole trail of broken hearts, used to getting whatever he wanted because of his family name, looks and money, not caring about anyone but himself. But she certainly hadn't met that guy. Maybe for a few minutes in the stables, right after they'd made love, when she'd thought he'd been dismissing her. She'd come to realize he hadn't been. He'd truly had to get back to his brother's wedding; he was a groomsman and was supposed to be there, not cavorting in the barn with a guest-slash-the-help. She'd been the one to insist they arrive back separately. And then what had he done? Asked her to dance quite a few times.

He'd also asked her for a no-strings romance.

And a platonic marriage.

So here was a truly great guy, sweet to babies and to the mother of his child, but who could not, would not, commit to a relationship.

So was he great or not great at all? The answer: not great for *her*. The more time she spent with Brandon, the more she liked him. No, she more than liked him. She was falling for him hard, despite all her warnings not to let that happen. But there was powerful stuff going on outside of her control.

He'd been her first love, even if it was just a few months of a high school romance and all they'd done was kiss. It made him special. Unforgettable. That he was so insanely good-looking and sexy, his dark eyes equally intense and playful, made him impossible to ignore. And that he was so thoughtful and made himself so available to her touched her deeply. She'd missed having "a person," someone who'd be there in a heartbeat for her, who'd drop everything if she needed them, as she'd do for them. Her "person" had always been her mom, and her loss had left a gaping hole inside Cassidy's heart that she hadn't even fully understood until Brandon Taylor came along and started filling it in.

"Someone's asleep," Brandon whispered, pointing a finger down at Maeve. He then brought that finger up to his lips in a *shh* gesture.

And somehow, that was all it took for a little voice inside her to say *I love you, damn it*.

Uneasy as that thought ping-ponged around her head, she bolted up. "I'll settle her in her bassinet." She reached out to take Maeve, but Brandon stood.

"I've got it," he said. "Transferring her to you and then to the bassinet might wake her. This way we skip a step." He looked at her for agreement, his dark eyes so warm it was hard to look away.

"Good point." She backed away, glad to have a moment to compose herself. *You don't love him, you just really like him. He's a surprise is all. And your baby's father. It's not love, it's not love, it's not love.*

Maybe she'd snap out of it by the end of the

night like Olympia Dukakis's character thought her daughter should do in the movie *Moonstruck*.

Cassidy led the way into her bedroom, where she'd had Tyler put the bassinet. Brandon easily settled Maeve, her little bunny beside her. The baby stirred, but then let out a sigh, her eyes remaining closed, her chest slowly rising and falling with her sleeping breaths.

"That went better than I thought," he said. "I'm not half bad at this."

She smiled. "Not half bad at all. Were you worried? Did you think she might barf all over you or that she'd scream every time you tried to hold her?"

"Yes, actually. I did. I never would have considered myself baby friendly."

"Me, either," she said. "But you're consistently full of surprises."

"In a good way, I hope."

She felt her smile fade. Not in a good way for her well-being. Or for her heart.

Once again he was staring at her, his gaze soft. He reached out a hand to her hair and tucked a swath behind her ear. "I hope our baby gets your eyes. So pretty."

She swallowed. She couldn't say anything.

He moved closer, the hand moving to her cheek. "So beautiful," he murmured.

You, too. You, too. You, too, she thought, unable

to take her eyes off his face. He was so close. And
so irresistible.

In moments she was backed up against the wall,
their mouths fused, his hands in her hair, hers on
his rock-solid chest.

She could feel him pulsating against her. All she
had to do was to keep kissing him, to keep touching
him, to say *yes*, and they'd be in her bed.

Back away from the hot man, she told herself.
*All getting naked with Brandon again will do is
leave you wanting more from him. And he's told
you he's not up for grabs.*

"You drive me wild, Cassidy," he whispered into
her ear, and she closed her eyes, giving herself a
few more seconds of such delicious pleasure.

But she couldn't exactly tell him they had to stop
when she was so busy kissing him.

Chapter Seven

Cassidy came to her senses in the nick of time, her T-shirt in a heap at her feet, his jeans unsnapped.

"Brandon," she said as his lips grazed her neck and his hands traveled across the lacy cups of her bra. "We can't do this. First of all, we're babysitting. What if Tyler and Callie stop by to pick up Maeve early and we're naked in bed? They asked me to babysit—not fool around while taking care of their daughter."

There. A very good reason to stop this craziness. They weren't in high school, making out on a couch while her little charge was fast asleep. They were adults and this was wrong on too many levels.

"Tomorrow night then?" he asked, reaching down to pick up her shirt for her.

She sighed and hurried into her T-shirt. "We'd better talk."

"My least favorite words," he said.

Her heart went south. This was the Brandon she'd been expecting all along. The one who wanted sex but not romance or love. The one who wasn't interested in the details, such as every messy step of what they'd gotten themselves into with the pregnancy. He was more big picture. She was pregnant, therefore he'd buy out pricey Baby Central in Lewistown and stash her in a luxe cabin on his property, wearing a wedding ring to a point, which would let him come and go as he pleased.

No sirree. Not with this woman.

She smoothed her hair and lifted her chin. He snapped his jeans.

She needed to make sure he understood that she was vulnerable to him—without saying it outright. She hated that he had the control here. He was the one who wasn't interested in a real relationship. Or love. She could either accept that or ignore it like an idiot, give in to her attraction for him, and end up potentially so hurt that it created a terrible rift between them. As parents, they couldn't afford that. They needed to be Team Baby.

So just stop it, Cassidy. You know how he feels. There's really nothing to talk about.

Except, as she watched him tiptoe over to the bassinet and check on Maeve, who was sleeping soundly, she was struck by the fact that this man had hidden depths he wasn't aware of. He could love; he simply chose not to. There was more to it than his family history. She'd experienced parental abandonment just as he had, but she knew her heart was open to love. Guarded, sure. But open to it. With the right person. Brandon was completely closed.

She suddenly realized that he must have been very hurt by previous romantic relationships. All that meant was that he'd been willing once to let himself feel *everything*. Therefore, he could do it again.

"Wow," he said, standing at the bassinet in the dimly lit room and looking down at the sleeping baby. "Look at that. Everything awaiting her, the entire world, all the possibilities."

Oh, Brandon. If it takes me every single day until my due date, I'm going to get that heart of yours back and running.

He turned just as she put her hands on her belly. Her expression must have been a mixture of a million things because he said, "A thousand pennies for your thoughts."

"Inflation or the Taylor riches?" she asked, shaking her head with a smile.

"Li'l of both."

"Just what you said. Our baby will have the whole world waiting for him or her. I want to do everything right by this little one." Suddenly, tears poked at the backs of her eyes. "I don't want to make mistakes and I know mistakes are easily made." She turned away, overcome by a burst of fear.

"Hey," he said, coming over and slinging an arm around her shoulder. "We're all human. No one's perfect, so yes, we're going to make mistakes. But mistakes can be healthy and teach us how to be better."

She nodded, the tears drying up. The man needed to take his own wisdom to heart.

"You're going to be a great mom, Cassidy."

A warmth spread inside her and she truly felt better. One minute he could make her feel there was no hope for them, and a second later, remind her that he just needed time to turn his heart around.

"Thank you. That means a lot to me. And you're going to be a great dad. I can see that in everything you do, Brandon."

"Am I blushing?" he asked, touching his cheeks with a twinkly-eyed smile.

He could be jokey all he wanted, but she knew she'd touched him as deeply as he'd touched her.

She did want to talk—though where the conversation would lead she had no idea—and doing so over dinner might help. "I have a ton of food, as you know." She headed to the doorway of her kitchen. "Want to try the lasagna?"

"I never turn down lasagna," he said with a bright smile. Trying to make nice, to make light. Diffuse the tension.

In the kitchen she poured herself a glass of her new decaf iced tea, took a gulp and instantly felt better. She poured another for Brandon and handed it to him.

He parked himself in a chair at the table, his gaze on her. "I guess we do have a lot to talk about," he said then took a long sip of the tea.

She let out a breath. "Yeah, we do."

He set the glass down on the table. "What do you *need*?"

"Need?" she repeated, glancing at him before reaching into the refrigerator for the container of lasagna.

"I just want to make sure I'm there for you. Here for you. I've been accusing of being dense when it comes to women and what they want. Or need. Maybe what you need is for me not to kiss you. Maybe you need a really solid friend. Whatever it is, I want to be there for you."

She really didn't know what to make of that. *Not kiss her. Solid friend.* She wanted him to fall for her the way she was falling for him, damn it. But clearly, he wasn't. "You've been very kind, Brandon. So—"

"Thanks, but what do you need from me?"

"That's hard to answer." It really was. If he proposed a real relationship, the two of them really trying to make this work because they were about to share a child, she would be all-in.

"I'm not sure what I need from you," she said. "You're here, you're committed to the baby." She bit her lip. She wanted a hell of a lot more than that.

"And that's what you *need*?" he asked. "Me to be there for both of you?"

"It's a little more complicated than that," she said, feeling a frown form. There was a whole universe in that question of his.

He looked at her, sort of biting his lip, his expression somewhat confused. What was he trying to get at?

"What I need is kind of a big question, Brandon. I mean...what do *you* need?"

He leaned back in his chair, hooking his thumbs into his jeans' pockets. "I guess it *is* harder to answer than it seems. Maybe you could just give me a list of tangibles. What you'd like to start getting for our baby. A bassinet like Maeve's, a crib, pj's, stuffed animals. Whatever you want."

Was that what he was talking about? *Stuff?*

"Need and want are different," she said, turning and sliding the lasagna into the oven.

"Are they really, though?" he asked when she spun around, his eyes steady on her.

"Yes. Very. There's a lot I want but don't need."

"Like what?" he asked.

She held back a sigh. She'd started this conversation and she just wanted to end it. They weren't on the same page. Or in the same realm.

"Come on," he said, taking a sip of his drink. "Like what?"

Fine. Though it annoyed her to explain something so basic that anyone who wasn't filthy rich would understand. "Like…the gorgeous, long red wool coat I saw in a shop window. That coat stops my heart every time I pass that shop. But it's *way* out of my budget. I have a perfectly nice wool coat already. And a down jacket. I don't need that red coat. I just want it. See?"

"But want can become need," he said. "I think if you want something bad enough, you begin to need it. You must have it."

She stared at him for a second. Yes, exactly. That was how she was beginning to think about him. But she had no idea what *he* was talking about. How it related to *them*. Unless she was giving him too much credit and he was thinking about a Range Rover or a trip to Tahiti. She got out two plates and utensils, her appetite diminishing by the second.

"Have you thought more about getting married?" he asked.

She whirled to face him. Was this the route he was on? How did want and need get him to this question? He didn't want or need to get married, not in the real sense.

You want to know what I need? To understand you. Just when I think I do, you throw me for a major loop.

"No. There's nothing to think about, Brandon." She sucked in a breath, remembering her conversation with Callie at Java and Juice about what a marriage would actually entail. "But tell me. Let's say we did get married. How exactly do you envision it? I mean, we wouldn't be a normal husband and wife. So we'd live together like roommates? Friends but sharing in the responsibility of raising our child?"

"Well, I guess I didn't think too far down the line. But it's a good question."

Aha. Didn't think it through. Once he did, he'd take back the proposal in a snap.

"What do you mean by roommates, exactly?" he asked—warily.

"Well, it would be a platonic marriage, right? So we'd be roommates. Housemates, I should say. We'd have separate bedrooms."

"But we'd be married," he said. Earnestly. "So, we'd share the master suite."

"Oh, the master suite," she sing-songed. "Brandon. Platonic couples, an oxymoron in itself, don't share bedrooms. Because they're not sleeping together. There's no sex."

He stared at her. "There could be."

Of course he expected sex. Brandon Taylor giving up all the hot singles of Bronco for a truly platonic marriage? No way. "So you see us married, having a sexual relationship, as married couples do, just without the emotional angle? It wouldn't be a love match. Is that it?"

She'd known from the get-go that love wouldn't be part of it. But she hadn't known he'd been counting on the shared bed.

"We already know how good we are together, Cass. Sexually."

"Didn't we have this exact conversation at the wedding? A no-strings romance? I said no thanks."

"Right," he said. "Except now we're expecting a baby. So it's a different conversation."

She laughed—but not happily. "I see. Now that we're having a baby, the conversation has morphed to *marriage* instead of just a *relationship*. Legally binding. Do you really believe any of this complete and utter crap you're saying?"

He frowned. "It makes sense to me, Cassidy."

No kidding. "It doesn't work for me. It's not what I *need*."

Fury whirred in her stomach. The smell of the lasagna was suddenly too much. She ran into the bathroom, thinking she had to throw up, but she didn't. She just needed to catch her breath. Splash some cool water on her face.

When she came out, Brandon was standing by the oven with her big yellow oven mitts. She'd heard the timer go off when she'd been in the bathroom, but hadn't had it in her to rush out. He took out the container of lasagna and began cutting and plating.

Ever helpful. Grr. *Be just one thing!* she wanted to scream like a crazy person. Of course, no one was or should be. But he needed to stop getting A pluses for kindness and generosity and thoughtfulness and Fs for relationships.

He brought the plates to the table and set them down. "I'm sorry, Cassidy. But I am who I am. I don't see myself changing. It took a lot to make me this way, and I'm fine with who I turned out to be."

She forced herself to sit. "Fine with not having a real relationship? How can you be so sure you'll love our baby if you can't love your wife?"

He stared at her, something shifting in his expression that told her she'd pushed a button he didn't want pushed.

She was about to apologize, to say that she knew full well there was a difference, but his phone pinged.

He pulled it out. "Oh, damn it. Text from my dad. There's a problem with Starlight. My favorite horse at the ranch. She's the one who eavesdropped on us talking the night of the wedding." He scanned the text. "My dad wants my help."

"Go," she said. "I think we could both use a break from our conversation anyway."

He nodded. "I'll take a rain check on the lasagna."

The moment the door closed behind him, she felt his absence so acutely that she had to sit and give herself a moment.

And she knew she'd already crossed her own line. There was no turning back from her feelings for Brandon. So she'd just put her energy to better use: turning *him* back from a life without love.

That somewhat settled, she dug into the lasagna. She was eating for two now, so she added his to her own plate.

"Let's go take the chocolate-coconut scones from the oven," Cassidy told Maeve, scooping the baby from the playpen in the kiddie section of Bronco Java and Juice. "You can take your bunny with you."

"La ba!" Maeve said, waving her new lovey.

It was six forty in the morning; the sky a beautiful dark pink and gray as the sun began to rise. Cassidy had been awake since just before five o'clock, when Maeve had let out a little shriek to let her sitter know she was ready to begin her day. Despite not having had a great night's sleep, thanks to some tossing and turning over her conversation with Brandon, Cassidy had excitedly rushed over to get Maeve, elated at caring for a baby and grateful for the practice.

She loved everything about the experience of caring for Maeve, from holding the sweet baby against her, feeding, changing, bathing, dressing, even getting spit up on. At one point, Cassidy realized she was talking to Maeve nonstop, detailing her every move, thinking out loud, and it occurred to her what good company a baby was, even if silent company.

One thing that had kept Cassidy awake last night was her quiet phone. She'd kept expecting it to ping with a text from Brandon, checking in, quipping about something, anything. But he hadn't texted at all. Maybe Starlight was very ill. Or maybe their conversation had been too much for him, as well. Granted, he would have left to help out at the ranch no matter what the two of them had been doing. Brandon wasn't a responsibility shirker. But he'd left very quickly and she'd been able to tell that he was relieved for the excuse to get out of there.

How can you be sure you'll love our baby if you can't love your wife?

She'd hit below the belt on that one. First of all, there was no wife and wouldn't be unless she agreed to his plan of *being* an unloved wife. She'd apologize when she saw him next, and she had no doubt she'd see him today. If she wanted to help

Brandon be able to love again, she had to be smart about it, not fling shaming accusations at him.

"Today's a new day, Maeve," she told the baby. "I'll start fresh with Brandon. What's my grand plan, you ask? To just be myself. To not talk so much about what's to come and what will be, and how this and how that, but just to *be*. Two people figuring things out as they go because they were thrown together into something huge. A you, Maeve. A baby." She scooped her up and twirled around, a rookie move when she knew better because a tiny fist grabbed the end of her ponytail and yanked.

"Oh yeah?" Cassidy said, giving the baby a tickle. Maeve giggled, her beautiful eyes twinkling. "And I have a much more fun activity for you instead of hair yanking. Let's go into the kitchen and take out the scones. Maybe we'll each swipe a piece. Yum!"

As she turned to put the baby in her stroller to wheel her into the kitchen, Cassidy had that funny feeling that someone was watching her. Not Maeve, who only had eyes for her bunny, which she was alternately shaking and chewing. Some *early* early birds outside awaiting their smoothies and lattes? Or maybe Tyler was a bit early to pick up his daughter? She expected him just before seven. Or perhaps Helen and Hank had arrived for their shift? Cassidy glanced at the glass front door, but there was no sign of anyone.

She was about to wheel Maeve behind the counter and into the kitchen when she had the feeling again. This time, she looked to the glass back door, which could be accessed from the kitchen and the shop.

Cassidy jumped. Winona Cobbs stood at the door, her razor-sharp gaze right on Cassidy. Ninety-four years old, Winona was a relative newcomer to Bronco. Cassidy had heard from Callie, who worked for Winona's great-grandson, that Winona was originally from a tiny town called Rust Creek Falls. She'd gotten pregnant as a teenager and had been told the baby had died and had then been separated from her beau, a man named Josiah Abernathy. But the baby girl had been alive the whole time. Thanks to sleuthing, caring folks, that baby had been located, and Winona had been reunited with her long-lost daughter, Daisy, with whom she now lived in Bronco.

Cassidy hurried through the kitchen and opened the door. "Morning, Miss Winona. We're not quite open yet, not till seven, but if you're wanting a quick cup of coffee or tea, I'd be happy to get you something."

"I've had my morning tea, thank you," Winona said. Her long white hair was in a ponytail down one shoulder of her purple tracksuit. "I was taking my morning stroll through the back nooks and crannies of the shops, and noticed you."

"Oh, well thanks for saying hi. Sure I can't get you a pastry? I have six kinds of muffins and three kinds of scones. Maybe a bagel? You can have your pick before the morning crowd shows up to devour them any minute now."

"I had sourdough toast and jam with my tea, so I'm just fine," Winona said. "But I'll tell you something, Cassidy Ware. You'll be glad you did it. Yes, you will."

Cassidy stared at the elderly woman. *Glad I did what?* she wondered.

Everyone said Winona was psychic and she did have her own business, Wisdom by Winona. Callie ran into Winona often since she worked for Winona's grandson at Bronco's Ghost Tours, where Winona had her shop in an office. Callie had told Cassidy that she'd come around to believing that Winona had a gift.

"What do you mean by that?" Cassidy asked Winona. "Glad I did what exactly?"

"You'll see. Oh yes, you will. You have a nice day now." Winona turned on her heel and walked away.

Cassidy tried not to frown. "You, too," she called. *You'll be glad you did it.* Did what?

She wanted to chase after Winona and demand

she answer the question. But she couldn't leave Maeve alone and she had to tend to the scones.

Did *what*? Was it something she'd already done? Or something she was going to do?

Hmm. Maybe Cassidy would make an appointment with Winona at her shop. Get an answer *and* have a formal sit-down reading of her fortunes, her future. Not that she necessarily believed in psychics. But she didn't *not* believe, either.

As Cassidy was coming to realize, anything was possible.

Chapter Eight

At seven in the morning, Brandon was finally ready for bed. The veterinarian had instructed him and the stable manager to watch the horse all night; she was having stomach issues, but neither Brandon nor the manager could figure out what the Appaloosa could have possibly eaten that could have resulted in this kind of colic. With Starlight more comfortable after getting some medicine, Brandon had settled in for the night in her stall, knowing full well he'd be unable to sleep a wink anyway. Not with that conversation with Cassidy knocking through his head. And not with all the reminders of where his present and future had begun. Right here.

He got up, pulled hay from his neck and hair, and rolled up the sleeping bag, talking gently to Starlight, who was much perkier this morning. He was about to text his dad that the horse was on the mend when he heard footsteps. One of the cowboys, Paul Fielding, came into view, holding the hand of a young boy, seven or eight at most. The boy was crying, his head hung. The cowboy looked grim. What was this about?

Paul nodded in greeting at Brandon then looked at the boy. "My son Kyle has something to say."

The boy's face crumpled and tears slipped down his freckled cheeks.

"Go ahead, Kyle," his dad said firmly.

The boy slashed two hands under his damp eyes, his shoulders shaking. "I didn't mean to make Starlight sick. I swear it!"

Ah. Mystery solved of how a horse with a restricted diet managed to eat something that made her so ill.

A teary-eyed, nervous Kyle looked down. "After school yesterday, I came to see her and Firecracker, my other favorite horse. And I had leftovers in my lunchbox so I gave them to Starlight. I'm really sorry," he added, the boy's remorse evident in his face and voice.

"Do you remember what you gave her?" Brandon asked.

Kyle nodded. "Apple slices. And the rest of my turkey and cheese sandwich. There was half left."

"Well, that doesn't sound too bad," Brandon said. "Definitely didn't agree with her, though."

Kyle hung his head again and scuffed the floor with one of his blue sneakers.

"Tell Mr. Taylor what else," his father said. "It's important he knows so that Starlight can get the best care."

Yeah, apple slices and a turkey sandwich, even the whole thing, wouldn't have gotten Starlight as sick as she'd been.

Kyle looked up, biting his lip. "There were a few Pop Rocks left in the pack, so I shook them out on my palm and held them out to her and she ate them. She seemed to like them. They were the cherry ones. I didn't know she'd get sick. I'm sorry." He burst into a fresh round of tears, the narrow shoulders trembling before he threw his arms around his dad's waist and buried his face in his hip.

"Kyle, you've got to face Mr. Taylor and your mistake," Paul said, his voice gentle but firm.

The boy slowly looked up at Brandon. "I'm really sorry. I'm sorry, Starlight," he called out to the horse.

Brandon knelt in front of Kyle. "The thing about horses is that, unlike people, they can't throw up or burp. So food that doesn't agree with them just stays in their bellies, making trouble."

Kyle wiped under his eyes again. "I didn't know that. Did you know that, Daddy?" he asked, turning to the cowboy.

Paul nodded. "I did, son. Animals and people have very different kinds of bodies. So you have to know what an animal can and can't eat before you offer it anything. If you want to work on a ranch someday, that's important to know."

"That's right," Brandon said, standing. "You want to be a cowboy like your dad, Kyle?"

Kyle nodded. "And I want to be a champion roper like Geoff Burris. He's my favorite. But my dad said I can't go to the holiday rodeo in November like we were gonna because of what I did to Starlight."

Brandon glanced at Paul, who looked pretty miserable himself. "Well, Kyle, you didn't know you would make Starlight ill and now you do. I'll bet anything you'll never feed the horses again without getting permission. Starlight was probably very happy to get those apple slices, but she can't have stuff like Pop Rocks."

Kyle nodded. "She did seem to like the apples best of all. My dad also said I'm not allowed to come in the stables anymore and I promise I won't."

Brandon slid a compassionate glance over to Paul, then looked at the boy. "Tell you what, Kyle. You obviously love horses, since you were just trying to share your lunch leftovers with Starlight.

She happens to be my favorite, too. If it's okay with your dad, it's okay with me for you come see her and any of the horses anytime you want. Just don't feed them without permission from a grown-up. Okay?"

Paul's shoulders visibly sagged with relief, and Brandon realized the guy was probably worried for his job.

Kyle's face broke into a smile. "Wow, thank you. I'm really sorry for what I did."

"I know you are," Brandon said. "Starlight's going to be fine. And I'm just glad she ate everything so that you couldn't give any Pop Rocks to Firecracker or we'd have had two horses with serious bellyaches."

Kyle's eyes widened. "Oh yeah. I'm glad, too."

"And," Brandon added, "if your dad thinks it's okay to take you to the rodeo to see Geoff Burris win again, like I know he will, I also think that's okay. Geoff's a Bronco hero."

"He's the best!" Kyle exclaimed. He looked at his dad. "Does that mean we can still go?"

"We'll talk about that on the way to school," Paul said, smoothing the boy's rumpled brown hair. "If Mr. Taylor's good with it, then maybe we can, after all. I know how much seeing your hero in person means to you."

"All right!" Kyle said and ran over to Brandon,

throwing his skinny arms around Brandon's hips for a hug.

Brandon grinned and gave the boy a squeeze.

After more apologies and a handshake from Paul, father and son headed down the long aisle, and Brandon heard Kyle say, "Daddy, Geoff Burris is my hero, but so are you."

Not much could bring a tear to Brandon's eyes, but that did. Funny, Cassidy was the one with all the new hormones coursing through her, and here he was, impending fatherhood making him all emotional.

He gave Starlight a pat on the nose and let her know he'd be back in an hour, then texted his father that the Appaloosa had come through fine and that the vet would be back around nine to check on her. He headed out of the stables, watching Paul and Kyle walk away holding hands, the boy's backpack dangling from one of Paul's shoulders.

That'll be me someday. Dealing with all the scrapes kids got themselves into. He thought Paul had handled the whole thing very well, and he'd be sure to seek him out later this morning to let him know. He tried to imagine himself with a child that age, helping out with homework, giving advice, going fishing, riding, hiking, and teaching them all about the ranch. Dragging the crying kid to apologize for this or that. He saw himself teaching his young daughter how to get up on a horse, her hair blond like Cassidy's, eyes dark like his. He saw himself helping his young son, his hair dark like Brandon's, eyes big and hazel like Cassidy's, with his math homework, then the three of them having dinner, walking the dog they'd adopt, talking about their days, sharing, laughing.

Fantasy? Or possible reality? He certainly hadn't experienced days like that with his own parents. He didn't remember his parents being married at all, though of course they had been. Maybe he was romanticizing a family scene because one didn't exist in his head. Therefore, the Norman Rockwell version was easy to make up. For all Brandon knew, he'd be a mediocre dad and say, *Sorry, I can't teach you to ride today, I have to work. Sorry, I can't help with long division, I need to make a business call.*

Nah. Brandon wouldn't be an "I'm too busy" dad. He'd be there one hundred percent, putting his child first. He'd felt that deeply from the get-go.

How can you be so sure you'll love our baby if you can't love your wife?

Cassidy's words from last night, right before his dad's text, slammed into his head. *Was* he romanticizing? Maybe Cassidy was right. If he couldn't stand the thought of commitment, didn't believe in a real marriage, what made him think he believed in the bonds of a parent and child?

Brandon stared out at the fence line, barely seeing ranch staff coming and going. He shivered as a chill snaked up his spine, though it was a perfect sixty-four-degree morning.

There was only one thing to do when Brandon's head got all turned around like this. Work.

Kyle Fielding had lit a fire under Brandon to call Geoff Burris and, for that alone, the kid deserved to go to the holiday rodeo. He headed into the main house, glad no one was around, and wound his way to his office. He'd focus on his job and his schedule and the word *love* would disappear from his head. He picked up his cell phone and scrolled his contacts until he reached Geoff Burris.

Time to get this done.

He pressed Send and waited.

"Okay," said a familiar deep voice, "my phone screen just told me Captain T was calling. I'm thinking the last time I had a captain named T was back in my sophomore year of high school, on the baseball team. Brandon Taylor?"

Brandon laughed. "I guess it's been a while since we've talked. Fifteen years. Though I've followed your career every step of the way. I'm a major fan, Geoff."

"Well, thanks. I'm doing what I love. What about you? I know from the rare times I get back to Bronco that you and your brothers all work for

Taylor Beef at the family ranch. Is that where you saw yourself back in the day?"

Had he? Working for the family corporation had forever been expected, and despite Brandon always forging his own path, he'd simply assumed he'd take his place at Taylor Beef. Obligation? Real interest? Family ties? He wasn't even sure he'd really ever thought about it, which was surprising in itself. Maybe it meant that the notion of family meant more to him than he'd been willing to consider. "I just saw myself working with horses, and I do spend a lot of time in our stables. Otherwise, I'm an executive VP for Taylor Beef. I like being part of the family business. Somehow I'm pretty good with number crunching."

"My team has been alerting me to your calls. Sorry I haven't personally called back. I'm pulled in a million directions every day and my schedule is nuts."

Brandon had no doubt. "Yeah, I bet. In fact, the man you've become, the champion you are, and your ties to Bronco are the reasons it would mean so much to Taylor Beef to have you promote our company in our new ad campaign, especially during the November rodeo. I hear you might be doing some promo shots for the rodeo and local TV and radio spots soon, so I'm hoping when you're in town, we can get together."

"You saying you don't have a date lined up for

every night of the week, Taylor?" Geoff asked on a laugh. "You can't tell me *the* Brandon Taylor has changed."

"I want to say I haven't. But things are complicated right now."

"Oh? Complicated is interesting. But maybe not for a guy who's used to playing the field. Someone's got you all turned around, huh?"

"I don't know, to be honest. But something is happening." He pictured Cassidy, hands on her belly... *Change the subject, Taylor,* he told himself. He had no idea what he thought or felt when it came to Cassidy Ware. "Your social life must be pretty amazing."

"I rarely have an evening to myself. Rodeos, promos, fundraisers, this event, that event. Everything seems to require a date, and yeah, there are plenty of very attractive women. Sometimes I love the life and sometimes I don't."

"I hear you," Brandon said. "All I know is that life is full of wild surprises."

Geoff let out a whistle. "Tell me about it."

"How about if I tell you more about why you should sign with Taylor Beef?"

Geoff chuckled. "You're good, I'll give you that. I've got five more minutes before I have to be at a press conference. Convince me right now to sign with you, and I'll let you know if you did by end of the week."

It was the only in he needed.

Brandon talked for a bit about what having a great man, hometown hero, and the roping champion of Montana as the Taylor Beef spokesman would mean to Brandon's father and uncles. He rattled off Taylor Beef numbers, family history, name recognition, product excellence, and talked about how Taylor Beef and the Taylor Ranch helped out in the community with fundraisers that benefited underserved ranching families in Bronco. How the ranch worked with the young cowboys and cowgirls associations of the county. Then he spoke of what Geoff meant to the company, to the town, to adults and children alike, and he told him the story of Kyle Fielding and Starlight. He even mentioned the boy managing to choke Brandon up with that hero comment.

When he finally stopped talking, he was 99 percent sure he'd done all the convincing he'd needed. Geoff even asked for the Fieldings' address to send them complimentary tickets and a T-shirt for both father and son. They ended the call, Geoff promising that his management team would be in touch by week's end with a decision.

I've got this in the bag, Brandon thought. But

that was always his problem. Overconfidence. Arrogance.

Nothing was guaranteed. Not signing Geoff Burris. Not getting Cassidy to agree to marry him. Not being a good father.

I'll tell you what your problem is, Brandon Taylor, you don't know how to love.

Elderly Winona Cobbs, with her snow-white long hair and purple cowboy hat, came to mind. He recalled her pronouncement before he'd snuck out of his brother's wedding.

Fine, he didn't know how to love. But you didn't have to learn to love a baby. That was automatic. He was—there was his overconfidence again—99 percent sure. Your child had your heart the moment you met him or her. That was how life worked.

Not for his mother. Not for Cassidy's father. But for most parents. Right?

Suddenly he wasn't so confident. He had *evidence* that he was wrong. In his own immediate family. Cassidy's, too.

He leaned back in his chair and put his feet up on his desk with a sigh.

Maybe he'd make an appointment at Wisdom by Winona. Ask a few questions. Talk through some of these burning issues. See what Winona said. If he *couldn't* love, then maybe he had no business being anyone's father.

Kind of late for that, he silently chided.

He was giving himself a headache. He thought he'd known himself so well until the bombshell of all bombshells had dropped on his head. Yes, a sit-down with Winona Cobbs, local psychic, might be just what he needed.

At twelve thirty that afternoon, Brandon peered at the turquoise wooden shed in the yard of Bronco Ghost Tours. Stars and crescent moons were painted on the rough planks. A sign hung on the purple door: Wisdom by Winona. Below it was another sign: Moved Inside Bronco Ghost Tours 'Til Summer.

Brandon glanced up at the bigger building and headed inside. He saw Callie Sheldrick at the front desk, but she was on the phone explaining about the various tours customers could sign up for. Bronco had a legendary history, and Evan Cruise, his sister's fiancé, had started a successful business that people flocked to. He held up a hand in greeting to Callie and she smiled. He peered at the doors down the hall. One was painted purple with crescent moons and stars. He warily walked over and knocked.

Winona Cobbs opened the door. Standing between two heavy purple drapes tied on each side, the elderly woman reminded him of an old-time rodeo queen. She wore a purple shirt with all sorts of colorful jewels on it, purple jeans, purple cowboy boots, and a purple turban on her head with a huge gold brooch in the shape of a crescent moon.

"Well, come on in," she said.

He peered in past her. Wasn't there a light in there? He stepped in and followed her through the drapes into a small room. Some illumination came from antique-looking lamps. The smell of incense infused the air.

"You may sit there," she added, pointing at a faded pink wing chair across from a purple one, which she sat on. A small table was between them.

"So how does this work?" he asked. "Do you use a crystal ball?"

She didn't respond. She was just staring at him. Not hard. No expression. Just staring. "Oh, Brandon. Brandon, Brandon, Brandon."

He raised an eyebrow.

She reached into a purple tote bag and pulled out a piece of purple paper and a pen, then jotted something down. "Here."

She slid the paper over to him. A scent wafted up to his nose. Lilac, maybe.

"'Lewistown Community Center,'" he read. "'Gwen and Paul Woodsley. This Thursday and Friday—9:00 a.m. to 12:00 p.m. Two hundred and fifty dollars per couple.'"

He looked up at Winona. "Uh, what's this?"

"It's a class for first-time parents," she said,

holding his gaze. "It covers pregnancy up to age two. Just right for you and Miss Ware."

He could feel his mouth drop open. He studied Winona for a moment. She had to be the real deal. How else would she *know*?

"I suggest you head over to Bronco Java and Juice right now and tell Miss Ware that you think the two of you should attend the parenting class. There's a lovely inn called the Blossom Bed and Breakfast where you can book a room for Thursday night. Tell the proprietor Winona sent you. She'll take care of you two real nice."

He tried to find words but his head was spinning. There was just too much to unpack here. "Let me ask you this, Miss Winona. You told me at my brother's wedding that my problem is that I don't know how to love. That may be true. So what's the point of any of this? I'm going to mess things up with Cassidy and I'll probably bomb at being a father, despite my intentions."

"I *also* said that the universe has something in store for you."

He hadn't forgotten; he just hadn't focused on that since it had sounded kind of silly. "I assumed the 'something' was the pregnancy. That I'm going to be a father."

"That's one of the somethings, yes."

One of them? "What else?" he asked.

"Brandon, I'd like to tell you that everything

is going to work out just fine for you. But when it comes to some people, they have to do the work first. You're one of those people."

"The work?" he repeated.

"The *work*. You've got to invest the time in yourself. If you want it, make it happen."

He tried not to sigh. "I thought this was supposed to be a psychic reading. I'm really just interested in knowing the end result."

A long-wrinkled finger came pointing at him. "You're a fine man, Brandon Taylor."

He waited. Surely that was the start of the sentence and more was coming. But Winona didn't say anything.

"You're a fine man," she finally repeated, frustrating the hell out of him. "And your sister is a lovely person. Happy to have her join the family. She makes my dear great-grandson Evan very happy." Winona stood.

He did, too. He'd go talk to Cassidy about the parenting class. Taking it certainly couldn't hurt. He'd likely come out of it feeling more prepared for what was to come than just reading about fatherhood could do for him. He could ask his questions, get real answers, unlike the kind Winona gave, and learn something. And he and Cassidy would do it together; they needed to come at this more united than they were at the moment. There was tension between them and he didn't like that.

He also liked the idea of staying overnight in Lewistown. Even in separate rooms, which he had no doubt she'd insist on. They could both use a couple of days away—for a lot of reasons.

He glanced at Winona, who was staring at him again, but this time, she wasn't expressionless or scowling at him.

"By George, I think he's got it," she said on a chuckle.

He gave her wrinkled hand a gentle pat of thanks and got out of there fast.

Chapter Nine

Cassidy had never been a clock-watcher. But today, closing time couldn't come fast enough. Since noon alone, it had been one little problem after another.

Two customers had gotten into a huge political argument and she'd had to ask them to take their ranting outside. She'd been met with applause from those who'd been listening to the raised voices. Then a toddler took his mother's cream-cheese-slathered bagel half and slapped it, facedown, on a velvet love seat. Once Cassidy had gotten that all cleaned up, a man dropped his red berry smoothie on the floor, missing one of the rugs by a few inches. A little while later, Cassidy had heard barking and had beelined for the back door, where she'd earlier set down a plate of kibble for the stray who might be Maggie, the lost dog from Happy Hearts, in the hope of attracting her. But by the time she'd gotten there, the dog was gone. As was the kibble. Darn.

For the past fifteen minutes, at least, nothing was going wrong. Two women dressed to the nines came in and ordered pricey green juices, full of compliments for how fresh the offerings were. Now this was more like it. Bring on the compliments.

As Cassidy stepped back to chop and slice and drop the veggies in the blender, she heard one of the women say Brandon's name. Naturally her ears perked right up. She moved around the side of the little island so she could eavesdrop better, knowing full well that she'd probably not like what she heard and should stand closer to the whirring blender.

"I still can't believe Brandon ghosted me last summer," the blonde said with a pout of her glossy lips. "We went out three times and he never called again. And *trust* me, I gave him reason to call." She ran a hand down the length of her excellent body.

Ugh, why did Cassidy think she wanted to hear this slop? Knowing Brandon had dated half the town's singles was bad enough. Listening to details of his sexcapades? No thanks. She moved closer to the blender.

And still heard every word.

Her brunette friend gave her a commiserating

smile. "Men are such dogs. Did I tell you I dated Brandon, too?" she asked, a faux sheepish expression on her pretty face.

"What? After I did?"

"Well, you said it was over so… I ran into him at a fundraiser my PR firm was working. He is so damned hot I couldn't help myself."

Double ugh. Take your juices and go!

"How many times did you go out?" the blonde asked as Cassidy came over with their orders, wishing she could plug her ears. Could this day get any worse?

"Twice. On our second date he took me to Coeur de l'Ouest, that excellent French restaurant just outside town, and he got all holier-than-thou because I told our waitress that the service was slow and that would be reflected in her tip. He had the nerve to say, 'Oh, are you planning to pay for this dinner?' We got into a huge argument and I huffed out."

"He probably asked *her* out right after you left," the blonde said, handing over her credit card.

Her friend nodded. "Right?"

Thank the heavens they took their juices to go. Cassidy had heard enough. Who hadn't Brandon dated in Bronco? Who hadn't he ghosted or dumped or pissed off in a fancy restaurant, even deservedly?

At least Brandon hadn't been going to undertip the waitress. That did not seem like his style, slow service or not, which was rarely if ever the waitstaff's fault.

Because he probably *had* wanted to ask her out, she thought with a scowl.

She wondered if she should even try chipping away at the bricks around his heart. The man was thirty-four and very likely set in his ways, used to living on his terms only, not having to account for anyone else. But now he did have someone else to account for: their child.

Chip away, she would. She owed it to herself and their baby to try. There was so much potential for them, if only he'd let her in. Maybe they'd be terrible together. Maybe they wouldn't work and they'd become a statistic like the ones he liked to throw around. But maybe they'd be great together. She just wanted a chance.

Cassidy looked at the clock on the wall. One forty-five. She couldn't wait to go upstairs, take a long, soothing shower, put on a face mask, and binge-watch the hot new regency romance series everyone was talking about. She was all caught up on her private baking orders, had started a nest egg and new business plan for her future expansion plans, and could just put her feet up and relax for the rest of the day. Ah. Just the thought of it made her feel better—and helped put Brandon Taylor, his trail of women and his antilove mindset out of her head.

"Hi, Cassidy!"

She turned to find her friend Susanna Henry smiling as she stepped up to the counter. Susanna was several years younger than Cassidy and an office manager for Abernathy Meats. Cassidy knew that Susanna had once dreamed of becoming an actress, and though she did volunteer at the community theater, Cassidy wondered if Susanna was happy. There was just something in her friend's expression sometimes—Cassidy couldn't quite put her finger on it

"I definitely need my caffeine fix," Susanna said, pushing her layered brown hair from her face and adjusting her long, filmy scarf. Susanna had great style. "I'd love a caramel macchiato."

Cassidy smiled. "Coming right up. How about a treat to go with it? There's only one chocolate-fudge cupcake left. So good."

"Oooh, I'll take it. I need chocolate to get me through the afternoon. I've been trying to get in touch with Geoff Burris all day and his team isn't returning my calls."

Cassidy held up a hand as she set Susanna's cupcake in a small box on the counter. "I'd better stop you there. I'm…friends with Brandon Taylor and he was talking recently about trying to get in touch with Geoff for Taylor Beef, so neither of us should say anything else. Conflict of interest or whatever."

"Definitely," Susanna said with a smile. "May

the best company win—which will be Abernathy Meats, of course."

Cassidy grinned. Susanna had been working for the company since high school, so she clearly had pride in her employer. Cassidy had always thought her friend had a little crush on Dean Abernathy, one of the five heirs to the Abernathy Meats company and the family cattle ranch. Dean was eight years older than twenty-five-year-old Susanna and, according to Susanna, he'd always treated her like the kid sister he'd never had.

A few more customers came in, so Susanna waved goodbye and left. Finally, it was two thirty and closing time, and Cassidy headed to the front door to turn the sign around. Ah, a little me time was definitely in order. This had been some day. On top of some night.

Just as she turned the sign, Brandon Taylor appeared in front of Java and Juice, holding up a hand in greeting. Surprised to see him, she opened the door, wondering what had made him stop by. Maybe just to check on her to see how she was feeling.

He looked too good in dark jeans, a white T-shirt, black leather jacket and cowboy boots.

"Have I got a story for you," he said, his dark eyes sparkling. "Firsthand, or I wouldn't believe it myself."

Cassidy tilted her head in curiosity, then walked

back behind the counter to start cleaning up. "A story?"

He closed the door behind him and followed her, stopping at the counter. "I made an appointment at Wisdom by Winona. Do you want to know what my fortune is?"

She gaped at him. He'd had a reading? Brandon Taylor? He didn't strike her as the psychic-reading type. "Yes, I really do."

"A parenting class in Lewistown. It's for both of us."

Okay, now she was really confused. "What? A parenting class?"

He launched into the story, from knocking on the purple moon-and-stars-painted door of Wisdom by Winona to the startling result of the reading: the class. "I was expecting having my palm read. A crystal ball. Tea leaves. And a real reading of my future. I mean, Winona sure looks the part."

Cassidy gasped. "Brandon, I just realized something. There's only one way Winona could have known I'm pregnant and that you're the father. If she's truly psychic. Only two people know in town—your sister and Callie. And I doubt either told a soul."

"Yeah, I thought about that, too. I'm sure they didn't tell anyone, so it's not like Winona could have heard about the pregnancy from gossip. So maybe there's more to this parenting class? Maybe the teacher is a wizard or something."

Cassidy laughed. A magic wand on Brandon would speed things along for sure. "Or maybe Winona is wise enough to know we could use a little help in all areas going forward—the class, some time away from Bronco and everyday life."

"Yeah, she also seemed to know what I was thinking at the end of our session, when I was sitting there trying to figure it all out." He chuckled. "So what do you think? Getting out of Dodge might be just what we need. I know I can use a parenting class, and being away will give us a chance to talk on neutral ground."

She nodded. "I'll need my own room at the B and B."

"I figured you'd say that. I'll register us for the class and call the inn the minute I leave here."

"Okay," she said. "Pick me up at seven forty-five on Thursday morning? That should give us time to get there and find the place."

"Will do." He held her gaze. "I have a good feeling about this, Cassidy."

She was too surprised to have a good feeling— yet. But she could use a parenting class, too. And some time away from Bronco. And the opportunity to work on Brandon Taylor in a neutral setting.

Yes. The more she thought about it, the more comfortable she became.

Excited, almost. If she would allow herself to go there.

And when she got back from the trip, she'd make an appointment with Winona herself. Who knew where she'd send her and Brandon next?

Last night, Brandon's father had a tirade when he'd heard that his executive VP was taking two days off—today and tomorrow—for personal reasons. Cornelius had demanded to know what those personal reasons were, but Brandon had been tight-lipped, which had infuriated his father even more. "That's *my* business," Brandon had said.

"Your business *is* my business," Cornelius had bellowed, but Brandon had reiterated that it actually was not, resulting in the stink eye, a finger jabbed at him, steam coming out of Cornelius's ears, and a tantrum about Brandon taking valuable time off to "gallivant around Lewistown."

Two words finally had made Cornelius not only calm down but change his tune completely.

Geoff Burris.

Brandon had assured his father that he expected positive news from Geoff about agreeing to sign with Taylor Beef for the ad campaign by tomorrow at the latest. Suddenly the man had been smiling and clapping Brandon on back saying, "You go enjoy yourself, son. You deserve some time off."

Now, as Brandon drove through the gates of the

Taylor Ranch at seven-thirty, he let out a relaxed sigh. He hadn't realized just how much he needed a break from his father's controlling ways and booming voice. Not that this trip would be a vacation, but Brandon sure was looking forward to it. To the class. The B and B. And spending two full days—and one long night—with Cassidy.

She was waiting in front of Java and Juice with a cardboard tray of coffees in her hand and a small suitcase beside her feet as he pulled up. She looked so pretty in black skinny jeans, ankle boots and a thick, long, off-white cardigan that belted around her waist. Her blond hair was in a loose bun, soft tendrils around her face. He wished he could kiss her hello. Maybe he could—on the cheek, anyway. But what he really wanted was a long, hot kiss, not a friendly kiss, and she'd already made it clear that friends was all they could be.

He parked and hopped out to open her door for her.

"Thanks," she said, sliding into her seat. "I made you a mocha latte and a mixed berry scone." She held up another bag. "I snagged a molasses cookie for myself—I had the strangest cravings for it this morning."

"Appreciated. I could use the caffeine boost," he said, taking a long sip before he set it into the console cup holder and pulled out of the spot. "What else do you find yourself craving?"

"All sorts of things. From soups—like the ones you brought me—to twice-baked potatoes with a ton of sour cream. And lemon zinger tea. I'm having that now." She took a sip, then set it in the other console holder and glanced out her window. "Wow, I can't believe I'm actually taking two days off. My trusty employee Helen will take over the front counter, and my part-timer, a hardworking community college student, will help Hank in the kitchen, so the place is all set. They're great staff."

"I'm glad you won't have to worry about your business. You can just focus on yourself, the class, doing some shopping in Lewistown, if you want, relaxing. Whatever you're up for."

She smiled. "Sounds pretty dreamy, actually. I owe Winona one."

"Have you seen her for a reading?" he asked as he turned onto the freeway.

"Not yet, but I've wanted to for a while. Part of me doesn't want to know what's to be. I mean, I'm not supposed to know till I get there, right? But part of me wants assurances. Then again, psychics don't give assurances—they give you truth."

"My truth is a parenting class?" he asked on a chuckle before taking a sip of his coffee, then another. It hit the spot. Between being on the road, having Cassidy in his car, and the caffeine, everything was A-OK right now.

"She must mean *something* by it. That's all she gave you? The date and time of a parenting class?"

"Well, at my brother's wedding, she told me my problem was that I didn't know how to love. So she got that out of the way already." He hadn't meant to say that. But it did sort of validate what he'd said the night they'd babysat, right before he'd had to leave. It was important to him that Cassidy knew he wasn't just making stuff up about his abilities—or lack, rather—on the subject of romance and relationships.

Her words echoed in his head.

So you see us married, having a sexual relationship, as married couples do, just without the emotional angle? It wouldn't be a love match. Is that it?

Yes, that was exactly it. And now a psychic had explained why. He didn't know how to love. He'd known how once, clearly. But he'd given all that up and so, at this point, he'd not only forgotten how to love, he planned to remain blissfully ignorant. For the rest of time.

And as he'd told Cassidy the night they'd looked after Maeve Abernathy, he was strictly talking romantic relationships. Not the parental one he'd have with his child. He believed there was a difference. But man, had that gotten Cassidy up in arms.

He felt her eyes on him. "Does Winona think the parenting class is an answer for that?"

"How could it be?" he asked. "What's the connection? It's just a how-to class for first-timers."

She seemed to be thinking that over. He glanced at her and could see her hazel eyes working furiously, pondering what he'd told her.

"A couple days ago," she said, "I found Winona staring at me through the back door at Java and Juice. She told me, 'You'll be glad you did it.' I asked her what she meant, but she wouldn't say. I mean, I do a lot of things all day long. What, specifically, will I be glad I did?"

"She's a cryptic one, that Winona Cobbs," Brandon said. "Frankly, she scares me a little. Maybe more than a little."

Cassidy smiled but instead of responding she took a long sip of her herbal tea, wrapping both hands around the cup. He sensed she needed some time to just sit and think, so he stayed silent. And so did she.

When they arrived in Lewistown at eight forty-five, the bigger town was bustling, people walking, jogging, window-shopping. Brandon used his maps app to find the community center. He parked in the back lot, and then he and Cassidy walked up the brick path to the double doors. He checked his registration receipt on his phone. Room 225. Inside, they took the elevator to the second floor and found the class.

A tall blond couple in their thirties stood at the

front of the medium-size room. The woman was pregnant, but Brandon had no idea how far along. Three rows of chairs formed a semicircle in front of a table they stood behind. There were all kinds of props on the table, from a weird-looking plastic contraption that Brandon didn't recognize to a few stuffed animals and bottles of laundry detergent. There was a basket with a sign reading *Class Syllabus. Take One!* Cassidy took two and handed him one.

He followed Cassidy to the second row, where she chose seats near the aisle. There were at least forty people of varied ages in the class; from a few who looked too young to be parents to a few in their fifties and sixties. Perhaps grandparents with responsibility for childcare needing a refresher. In any case, Brandon appreciated being one of many instead of a smaller, more intimate group where the teachers might make him talk. He was about to scan the syllabus, but one of the teachers started speaking.

"Welcome!" the blond woman said. "I'm Gwen Woodsley and this is my husband, Paul Woodsley." She touched her belly. "As you can see, I'm expecting. I'm six months along and due right around Christmas. We also have a fourteen-month-old, an adorable girl who just started to walk, so whether you're expecting or have a baby, we've got you covered."

So far, so good, Brandon thought. The teachers were right there in the trenches.

Gwen nodded. "Now, if you look around the room, you'll see a varied mix. Single parents-to-be. Divorced. Partners who are not married. And married couples. No matter the type of family you'll form, first-time parenting can be challenging."

Paul then went on to describe those challenges, some of which Brandon had never thought about. Such as: if you're divorced or not married but sharing custody, who gets the child on Christmas? Who gets the child on his birthday? Making those kinds of choices couldn't be easy, Brandon figured. He made a mental note to tell Cassidy that it was exactly one of the reasons they should get married. Neither would be away from their child on holidays. Neither would miss their kid's birthday.

"Okay," Gwen said with a clap of her hands. She went on to describe needing a support system in every sense of the word.

There were murmurings of agreement.

Brandon made a running list of who he could call in an emergency. His dad and Jessica in a heartbeat. And they'd come running. Interesting and unexpected, he thought. But the truth. And his siblings. Each and every one. He had some good friends he could count on, too. He sat a little straighter, already feeling more in control now that he had that vital aspect covered.

He felt Cassidy's eyes on him and turned to her, but she shifted her gaze straight ahead toward the teachers. Her expression seemed a little...stony.

"I want you all to take out your syllabus," Gwen said, "and a pen. And I want you to underline the heading of paragraph one—Support System."

He watched Cassidy underline *Support System*. He wondered what hers was.

"Okay, next, this is for all of you who are expecting," Paul said. "Three-quarters of you." He went on describe the importance of reading and research, knowing what foods were toxic to pregnant women, seeing your OB for prenatal checkups and taking prenatal vitamins. "Your syllabus has a list of no-no's and super yeses—but your homework is to read up on those lists and the reasons behind it."

Brandon was writing furiously, taking more notes in the past twenty minutes than he had in all of high school combined.

Cassidy turned to face him. "I like that you're taking the class seriously."

He held up two fingers. "Scouts honor that I will give up Caesar dressing—a no-no for pregnant women—on my salad in solidarity."

She laughed. "You don't have to do that."

"Yes, I do."

For the next hour and a half, the Woodsleys talked about how to know it was time to call your doctor and go to the hospital, how to time contractions, that there was something called false contractions. They talked breastfeeding and formula, how to care for the umbilical stump, when to introduce solids, teething, self-soothing, sleep schedules. Brandon's head was beginning to spin. Finally, the Woodsleys called for a fifteen-minute break, noting that light refreshments were on the buffet table at the back of the room.

"I seriously need coffee," Brandon said. "My third cup of the morning."

"I wish I could have caffeine. But I'll settle for decaf. It'll trick my brain."

They made their way to the back of the room, waiting in line for the refreshments table.

"So, how are you finding all the info?" Cassidy asked. "It's a lot."

"I feel like my head must have expanded by five sizes—that's how much new information is stuffed inside. And we're only halfway through the first day." He slapped a palm to his forehead. "But seriously, I'm getting a lot out of the class. I didn't know three-quarters of this stuff."

She nodded. "A lot is new to me, too. I don't have a ton of experience with newborns. And, um, the, *umbilical stump*? What?"

"Right?" he said with a conspiratorial smile. "You can be in charge of that."

"Well, you'll have to be when the baby is with you."

"Not if we get married," he whispered.

"Brandon. We covered that."

They reached the coffee urns and made their drinks, Brandon adding an extra pack of sugar for the rush or he might not survive the second half.

Based on everything he'd heard so far, convincing Cassidy to marry him was now number one on his to-do list. Who *was* her support system? She didn't have family.

And if they got married, they could trade off tasks. She would take care of the umbilical cord stump with the alcohol-soaked cotton balls, and he'd do the bathing, breathing in that baby-shampoo scent.

He had to convince her. And he had this entire little trip to do it.

Chapter Ten

After class was dismissed for the day at noon, Cassidy suggested having lunch first and then heading to their bed-and-breakfast, since check-in time wasn't until two o'clock.

"If you still have a craving for that twice-baked potato," Brandon said, "I know a great bar and grill that has them. And a little bit of everything."

"Sounds perfect." After that information overload, Cassidy wanted comfort food and then a nap.

He held out the crook his arm and she was so touched by the gesture that she stopped walking for a moment. She looped her arm around his. How long had it been since she'd walked down the street like this with a man? Forever. Part of a pair. Coupled. And this time, with the father of her baby. She was already deeply drawn to Brandon, but their connection made it all the more powerful.

An hour and a half later they'd finished lunch, Cassidy with a happy belly full of a healthful green salad with pregnancy-cleared dressing and a scrumptious twice-baked potato with extra sour cream. She'd been unable to resist trying one of Brandon's onion rings, and she wasn't surprised that he was a sharer.

Close to two, they arrived at their bed-and-breakfast, a charming Victorian just a couple of blocks off the main street but tucked away in its own private circle of huge trees. Following her into the inn, Brandon had his duffel slung over his shoulder and Cassidy's small, wheeled suitcase.

She headed for the front desk and the smiling woman behind it, who introduced herself as the proprietor, Amy Peterman. Cassidy gave their names.

Amy typed at the tablet in front of her. "There's a reservation for one room for Brandon Taylor. I don't see a reservation for a Cassidy Ware, and I'm very sorry, but we're fully booked."

Cassidy narrowed her eyes at Brandon. Had he only booked one room when she'd made a point of saying she wanted her own?

He stepped up to the desk. "When I called two

days ago to make the reservations, I asked for two rooms and was told I was all set."

The woman frowned. "By any chance, did the person you spoke to sound like a bored teenage girl?"

Brandon raised an eyebrow. "You know, now that you mention it, kind of."

"Sarah Peterman!" the woman called toward a room behind the desk. "Come out here."

A girl around sixteen came out. "Oh my God, what did I do now, Mom?"

Amy had her hands on her hips. "Two days ago, when I asked you to cover the phone for me for a half hour, did you take a reservation for *two* people, Brandon Taylor and Cassidy Ware, and then only enter one reservation?"

The girl tilted her head. "I do remember the name Cassidy. The new girl at school is named Cassidy. I like it."

Her mother stared at her. "You entered only *one* reservation for *one* of them."

The girl grimaced. "Sorry. I waited to enter the reservations until after I disconnected because I hate having to hold the phone against my ear while I type, but then the phone rang again and I got distracted. I'm really sorry."

Amy sighed. "And *I'm* really sorry," she said, turning back to Cassidy and Brandon. "We do only have the one room. The good news is that it's one of our largest and has a king-size bed."

Now it was Cassidy's turn to sigh. To Brandon, she said, "Ever see that old movie with Clark Gable and Carol Lombard when they hang a sheet between their sides of the bed? That'll be us."

"You take the room," he said. "I'll find a room somewhere else. You go relax, and I'll be back in a jiff."

The proprietor shook her head. "Oh, you won't find a room in Lewistown this week. Three conventions in town. Everyone's thrilled to be booked solid."

"It's okay, Brandon," Cassidy said, maybe a little glad that they were forced to share a room. Maybe some intimacy—of the close proximity kind—would work a little magic on him.

Amy showed them to their room, insisting that her daughter, Sarah, be the porter. The girl scowled but complied, carrying their bags ahead of them up the short flight of steps to the second floor.

The room was lovely. Big and airy, with a sliding-glass door that led to a balcony holding a small café table and two chairs. Soothing pale blue walls with watercolors of the mountains and a couple of Montana landmarks. A huge, white-wood four-poster with a soft down comforter and a ton of pillows. A side table holding a welcome basket and bottles of water.

When the proprietor and her daughter left, Cassidy kicked off her boots and tried the bed, the pillows so cuddly.

"Ah, heaven," she said. She was about ready for that nap.

"Mind if I try?" he asked.

"Go right ahead."

She was never so aware of anything as when Brandon lay beside her, both of them looking up at the beamed ceiling.

"Very comfortable," he said, turning his head toward her. He was so tall and strong and…sexy.

Do not look at him or you will want to kiss him, she ordered herself.

"So, what's on the agenda for the rest of the day and night?" he asked.

"Definitely a short nap in this amazing bed," she said. "Then maybe we could go exploring. I haven't spent much time in Lewistown."

"Sounds like a plan. You nap and I'll read the longest class syllabus I've ever seen. I want to be prepared for tomorrow so I'm not scared out of my mind."

She laughed. "Were you overwhelmed today?"

"Maybe just a little. Or a lot."

"I was, too," she admitted. "But now that I'm here, on this insane bed with this amazing down comforter, all the info is gelling and clicking instead of stacking."

"Maybe that'll happen for me if I close my eyes." He did, and she smiled. "Nope, just stacks upon stacks of information about bottle nipples and diaper sizing."

He turned onto his side, propped himself up on his elbow and faced her, tucking a strand of her hair behind her ear.

She froze, almost afraid of his touch, of wanting him so bad she might grab him and pull him to her.

"I'm glad we're here," she whispered.

He reached for her hand and found it and held it, the warmth so comforting that she relaxed and felt herself drifting off.

When her eyes opened, the room was dimly lit, and Brandon was sitting in the club chair at the desk, reading the class syllabus. She glanced at the alarm clock on the bedside table. She'd been sleeping for almost an hour. Had he been reading this whole time? She smiled at the thought.

"Give me ten minutes to make myself presentable, and we'll go explore," she said.

He turned with that smile that always went straight to her heart. "I told you in the stables, Cassidy. You always look beautiful."

Aw, God. Stop making yourself so necessary to me, she wanted to say, But she was tongue-tied. She slipped out of bed and rummaged in her suitcase for jeans and a sweater and her toiletry bag, then headed into the bathroom, which was practically the size of her apartment's bedroom. Every amenity was on the counter or bolted into the wall. And two fluffy white spa robes hung on the back of the door. Oh yeah, she would definitely be wearing one of those later.

She washed her face with the delicious-smelling soap, patted her face dry with a soft, thick towel, then put on a little makeup, brushed her hair, and changed into the fresh clothes. Ah, she felt so good now.

When she came out, Brandon was sitting on the edge of the bed with a very large plastic shopping bag with BH Couture written across it. Only the most exclusive, expensive clothing boutique in Bronco Heights.

"Bought yourself a pair of jeans?" she teased.

"No, socks. For a hundred bucks."

"Actually, this is for you," he said, standing and holding out the bag.

"For me?"

She took the bag over to the bed, set it down, and opened it up—and gasped. She pulled out The Coat. The long red wool coat that she'd fallen in love with in the window of BH Couture but would never in a million years be able to afford.

"Brandon." That was all she could manage to say.

"I happened to pass the boutique and notice this coat. It looked just like you described it the other day, so I went in and asked the saleswoman if she happened to notice anyone stopping to ogle this coat. She said that Cassidy Ware stops in front of the window almost every day and stares at it with a dreamy expression, but never comes in."

Um, a little embarrassing. "Who noticed me?"

"Sofia Sanchez," Brandon said. "My new sister-in-law's sister."

You mean your ex-girlfriend. She knew the two had dated, but she really didn't know if they'd been serious or not. Then again, did Brandon get serious about any woman?

"Brandon, you can't go around buying me expensive coats."

"Why not?"

She knew how much this coat cost. A lot of smoothies and lattes. Months' worth. "Because it's not a normal gift. And there's no gift required. It's not my birthday."

"I just wanted to do something nice for you, Cassidy. Besides, the weather's turned a bit. It's fifty-five degrees. Now you'll be warm enough."

She bit her lip and stared at the gorgeous coat, such a perfect shade of deep red, such fine wool. She loved it so much.

"At least try it on," he said.

She did. And once it was on, she was never, ever taking it off. She went to the ornate wrought-iron floor-length mirror attached to the wall and buttoned it, then tied the belt around her waist. "I love it to pieces."

He smiled, and she walked over to where he stood by the bed. She lifted her face to kiss him on the cheek but he turned at that exact moment and their lips met instead.

"Thank you," she whispered. "I feel a little bit like Cinderella right now. But I'll tell you, Brandon Taylor, I'm my own fairy godmother. You hear me? I don't need a prince. I love this coat and I'm sleeping it in, but no more gifts, okay?"

"Okay," he said, leaning forward and capturing her mouth in another kiss. Her knees went slightly weak and she was so intoxicated by him that she didn't pull away.

"None of that, either," she said, stepping back.

He didn't respond, just smiled, and she knew she was in big trouble here. She loved this room. She loved her coat. She loved *him*.

I love you, Brandon Taylor.

There it was. The truth. And once Cassidy admitted something to herself, she was stuck with it. There was no going back from this. That meant she had her work cut out for her.

After walking around Lewistown, window-shopping and going in and out of shops, Cassidy looking so beautiful in her red coat, they decided to bring takeout back to the inn and call it a day.

Brandon had heard raves about a Mexican restaurant named Manuel's, so they picked up burritos, chips and salsa, and walked back to the Blossom Bed and Breakfast, where teenage Sarah was behind the desk, typing away at her own phone instead of answering the ringing inn phone. Her mother came out from the back room, muttering her daughter's name.

Brandon chuckled as they took the stairs. "When our daughter is a teenager, she'll answer the phone." He fit the old-fashioned key into their room door. "She'll be one of those perfect teenagers who's never sullen, always smiles, does her homework, doesn't date till she's twenty-one."

Cassidy laughed. "Honestly, I can't imagine the baby any older than six months. Past that is too scary. Teething? Walking? It's all too much!"

Once inside, Brandon took off his leather jacket and hung it up, but Cassidy wrapped her arms around herself.

"If I wasn't so nervous about black beans and salsa falling out of my burrito and onto my coat, I'd keep it on while we eat. But I can't risk it." She took it off. "Bye, my beauty."

He smiled as she hung up her coat beside his. He loved how happy the coat made her. "A bit too cold to eat on the balcony," he said, setting their food and their drinks on the small table by the window.

They sat and dug in, both agreeing that Manuel's was delicious. Even the tortilla chips were unusually good, light and crisp with a hint of lime.

Cassidy took another bite of her veggie burrito then a sip of her water. "So, after everything we learned today at class, I think we should talk about how we see things working when the baby comes. I mean, since we're not getting married."

"Or we could just get married," he said, swiping a chip through the excellent salsa.

She moved her burrito from in front of her face to stare at him, a slight frown on her beautiful forehead. "We can't. I told you, I'm holding out for true love, Brandon."

His stomach churned. True love. *Come on.* Hadn't she been through enough herself? Maybe she hadn't. "Are you telling me that after your own failed romances, you still believe in love?"

Cassidy nodded. "I learned something from those failed romances. So, yes."

"Like what?"

She sipped her water, then set down the bottle. "Well, with my most serious relationship, I learned that I give it all I have until I know it's hopeless. That's both good and bad. I fell hard for a guy who really couldn't love. I didn't understand that at first, though. I thought he was just not demonstrative. I overlooked a lot because I thought he was a very busy ER doctor, dedicated to his work."

"So you understand, then. I mean I'm sorry you

had to go through that, but you understand why I stay uninvolved from the start. That way, no one gets hurt."

"There's a big difference between Dr. Dead Inside and you, Brandon Taylor. He was a true cold fish. You're the opposite of that. You're warm and kind and thoughtful. He never would have brought me soup or remembered my mentioning a coat I loved in a shop window."

"I don't have to be dead inside to know relationships never work out." He took another bite of his burrito, thinking of how to change the subject without her noticing. "Did you know that by the end of the first month of pregnancy, babies are a quarter inch long? So tiny!"

Yeah, nothing obvious about that change of subject.

She was staring at him, but didn't respond.

"I brought my fatherhood book with me and was reading while you were napping earlier," he explained. "I like knowing what's going on in there," he added, gesturing at her stomach. "I highlighted a few areas I wanted to ask the Woodsleys about tomorrow."

She put down her burrito and cleared her throat, then her gaze was back on him. Intensely. "The other day, you asked me what I needed, Brandon. Remember that?"

He sat back in his chair, slightly worried where this was going. "I remember."

"Do you want to know? Really want to know? Because I know the answer now."

Oh hell. What if what she wanted wasn't what he wanted? What if the one thing she wanted was the one thing he couldn't give her? Even with all his money.

But he couldn't deny that he did want to know. He wanted to know everything about Cassidy Ware, even the harder-to-deal-with stuff. "Yes, tell me. I don't want secrets between us. Everything should be out in the open."

"Good. It means a lot that you feel that way. So here it is—what I need. A *real* relationship with you. I want you to try. We're going to have a baby, so we're going to be in each other's lives forever. I have feelings for you and I know you have feelings me. So let's see where we can take this. You want to get married without love for the sake of the baby? Let's try a real relationship for the sake of the baby. There, I said it." She let out a breath. "And trust me, that wasn't easy, given your stance."

Brandon shook his head and stood, his stomach really twisting now. "I'm not willing to destroy things between us, Cassidy. Our relationship— as our baby's parents—is too important. My own parents aside, I had some friends growing up with divorced parents who hated each other's guts and used their kids as pawns. I'm not going there, Cassidy."

"So you can't even imagine that we'll work out? That we'll be one of those elderly couples on a porch, sharing a glass of sweet tea and waiting for our great-grandkids to come over?"

"Statistics say we have a fifty-fifty shot," he reminded her. "Those are crap odds. You want to risk us hating each other when we have a child to raise? I don't want to make trouble for my kid. I don't want strife in my own house. There's enough of that in the world."

She looked so frustrated that he told himself to shut up and sit down.

"How do I fight this?" she asked, her voice cracking. "How do I get you to see that some risks are worth it when everything you're saying isn't wrong?" Tears shone in her eyes and she shook her head, turning away from him.

He knelt in front of her and took her hands. "Cassidy, are you kidding me? Being here with you is a risk. Seeing you every day is a risk. I've never cared about anyone the way I care about you."

She swiveled and looked at him.

"There, I said it," he added with a gentle smile. "And trust me, that wasn't easy, given my stance."

His stealing her line got a small smile out of her. She squeezed his hand back, a good sign.

"What if we *try*," she said, "and at the first sign

that we're not meant to be, we agree to our old high school bet—to go our separate ways forever, romantically speaking. I think we'll know pretty fast if we're not a real match, Brandon. Right now, we've got something really huge in common and it's running the show in terms of a relationship. So let's find out if we have the fundamentals in common. Let's find out if we can really talk to each other. Let's find out if we're good together."

Something inside his chest untwisted and twisted, untwisted and twisted. "Damn it, Cassidy. Stop making it impossible for me to tell you no."

"If you want to give me what I need, this is what I need. Your willingness to try us out."

He stood and reached out a hand, and she looked at him with so much hope in her eyes. She stood, too, and he pulled her against him, holding her close. "Okay," he finally said.

But now his chest was tightening in on itself. Squeezing. This was a mistake, he knew. They were headed for heartache and everything was going to fall apart. He was going to disappoint her and then his doomsday predictions for joint custody would come to fruition.

But how could he not try when she was asking? Because everything *she* was saying wasn't wrong.

She tightened her hold on him, resting her head against his chest. *Just go with it and maybe you'll be proved wrong*, he told himself. *For right now, put it out of your mind and just enjoy Cassidy in your arms.* He could stand like this for hours.

"When I'm a hundred and two and look back on my life, this moment will be one of the tops, Brandon."

He tilted up her chin with his hand. "Guess it's okay for me to kiss you now."

"Yup," she whispered. "And more."

"That does sweeten the pot," he said.

She unbuttoned her cardigan slowly, her gaze on his, and tossed it to the chair. She wore a tight, silky black cami with lace at the V-neck. He lifted that off her in seconds. As he kissed her neck and made quick work of her sexy black bra, she wriggled out of her jeans and then unsnapped and unzipped his.

"You might have waited to ask me to try *now*," he said. "I would have promised you anything for this."

"First of all, we wouldn't have gotten this far right now without your yes. And I'll always know I got it out of you without getting you all hot and bothered," she whispered, a hand slipping into his boxer briefs.

He back-walked her to the bed, kissing her sexy pink-red mouth and neck en route, and all thought was replaced by pure sensation. Then he was under the covers with a naked Cassidy, the ends of her silky hair tickling his chest as her hands and mouth moved down his body.

As she slid back up his body to kiss him, he was half-aware that this felt different, *was* different from the first time just weeks ago. Back then, he'd whispered that she was "everything," and he'd meant *in that moment*.

But now, Cassidy Ware was everything in every moment. Now. An hour from now. Tomorrow. Eight months in the future when they'd have a baby. Forever. He *did* care about her more than he was willing to dig into. She was going to be the mother of his child. She had his full attention, and not just because her tongue was roaming across his lower belly.

He wanted to stop thinking so he kissed her, hot and passionately as his hands explored every inch of her soft body. He nudged her over so he was on top, and when he looked at her, his beautiful Cassidy naked before him, he was hit by a rush of feeling so startling that he blinked against it. He clasped both her hands and brought them up past her head, trying not to think as he kissed her neck, then lingered on her breasts, then licked his way down her torso.

"Oh, Brandon," she murmured, writhing. Moaning. Arching her back.

It took every bit of control not to enter her. If he did, it would be over way too soon.

But if he waited, he'd be aware of how his heart was beating too fast, of the fullness in his chest—a good fullness. Because Cassidy was in there.

He could talk about statistics all he wanted, but the way he felt was a fact, too.

Scary as hell.

She wrapped her arms around him as she pulled him up her body, her nails slightly digging into his back, her lips on his neck, her tongue dangerously close to his ear.

And then he couldn't wait a moment longer. He had to be one with her.

"Brandon!" she whisper-screamed as he moved against her, slow at first, driving them both wild if their muffled moans were any indication. Then faster, faster, faster, building, building, building.

When he was one hundred and two and looked back on his life, he knew this moment would be tops for him, too. Not the sex, though he could barely control himself. But the okay, the yes, that he was going to try.

Chapter Eleven

Cassidy woke the next morning alone in the king-size bed. She sat up, listening for sounds of the shower running. But the room was silent. And dark. Brandon wasn't in the club chair, reading. He wasn't *there*.

Her heart plummeted and she lay down slowly, closing her eyes. *Fool, fool, fool*, she thought. *Of course he's gone before dawn.* He might have meant his *okay* yesterday—and she knew he meant it while they were having incredible sex—but he probably woke at 4:00 a.m., hyperventilating, and headed for the hills.

Fine, she thought, straightening, determined not

to let him make her miserable and ruin her day. She would get herself up, showered and dressed, and go have breakfast downstairs. Inn breakfasts were the best. Then she'd go to part two of the class and somehow get herself back to Bronco. Surely, Brandon wouldn't have stranded her here, though. No, he'd never do that, no matter how freaked out he was about saying yes to a real relationship.

What was she doing? Why was she reading the worst into him being gone? If they were going to have a real chance, she needed to have more trust in him. She turned on the bedside lamp and there it was. The note it hadn't even occurred to her to look for.

Friday, 6:15ish

Went down to get coffee for us. We can have breakfast here or go to the diner we passed yesterday. If Sleeping Beauty wakes up in time before class.

—B

That sludgy feeling in her stomach dissolved. *You know him better than you think you do. Trust what you're doing to work and it will.*

She dashed into the shower, recalling every moment of last night. At first he'd been a little too gentle until she showed him he didn't have to be. They were a match in bed and out of bed. They could talk about anything. They found the same things funny and *not* funny. They were going to have a baby.

They were meant to be. She believed that. And now that they were a couple, he would come to see that in no time. She knew she would hit a roadblock or two when he'd feel overwhelmed, and she'd deal with it, get him through it. Hey, if he was so over-come with emotion for her that it tripped him up, wasn't it her job to help?

Cassidy smiled as she stepped onto the bath mat and toweled off, then put on that fluffy spa robe. Heavenly. When she came out of the bathroom combing her hair, Brandon was back, sitting at the desk with two foam cups of coffee in front of him.

"You should have waited," he said. "Now you're just going to get all dirty again."

For a second she had no idea what he meant, until he walked over to her and untied her robe, his hands roaming as he kept his dark eyes on hers. She had to close hers, she was so lost in desire for him. Before she could even process it, his clothes were off and they were back in bed.

An hour later, she had her second shower of the morning, but this time not alone.

"So far, I'm okay with having a real relationship with you," he said as he put on his own fluffy robe.

She fake socked him in the arm. "I admit I'm having a grand old time myself."

He hugged her to him. "Now I'm ravenous for food."

She grinned. "Me, too."

At just past eight they were downstairs in the dining room. Four tables were occupied by other guests, so Cassidy chose the small round one by the side window. Amy was running between the tables, serving plates, refilling orange juice glasses. Her daughter, Sarah, appeared with her backpack and a muttered, "Bye," as she headed for the door.

"Sarah Peterman, you come here this instant," Amy called out.

Sarah groaned. "Oh my God, Mom, what did I do now?" That was definitely her favorite refrain.

"Let me give you a kiss goodbye," Amy said, hugging the girl to her. "I've barely seen you all morning. Have a great day, honey."

Sarah brightened and grabbed a scone from the basket on the buffet table. "Bye, Mom."

Cassidy grinned at Brandon. "I think those two are a lot closer than they let on."

"Were you close with your mom?" he asked.

She waited to answer until Amy had poured their coffee and taken their orders for the special— French toast with cinnamon sugar.

"We were, but my mom was busy, like Amy," she whispered. "I was on my own a lot. I think it made me more independent. My mother was very supportive of my goal to have my own business. For some reason, opening a shop in Bronco Heights seemed like the height of making it when I was in high school. To her, too."

"Because you lived in Bronco Valley then?" he asked.

She nodded. "I was surprised that you deigned to date a Valley girl. The two sides of town didn't really mix much back then."

"I liked you, and that's all I needed to know," he said.

She reached for his hand and gave it a squeeze. She loved so much about him. She loved *him*.

"I was only at your house a couple of times since your mom didn't exactly approve of me, but I do remember wondering how you two fit in that tiny place. There was only one bedroom."

"My mom insisted I take it. I was so blind back then, I didn't realize how much she was sacrificing. She should have had the private room and instead she slept on a pullout in the living room." She shook her head. "I always dreamed that one day I'd be able to buy her a pretty house in Bronco Heights. She thought moving to the Heights meant she'd made it." She felt tears prick her eyes and she blinked them away.

"You still own that house in Bronco Valley?" he asked as Amy set down their French toast.

Cassidy shook her head. "When my mom was very sick, she told me to get rid of it once she was gone and use the sale money to start my business. The house sold for peanuts and I had to take out a small loan to get Bronco Java and Juice started, but I knew I was making her proud in heaven. To the very end, my mother was my biggest champion and support system. God, I miss her."

"Your mom sounds like an incredible person."

"She was. And though I do know she'd be proud of me, I also feel like I let her down. It's been five years since I opened the shop, and I really thought I'd have expanded—a sidebar in a fancy hotel in one of the cities or a second location."

"What's keeping you from expanding?" he asked, swiping a bite of cinnamon-sugar-dotted French toast in syrup.

"Well, I'd been hoping to expand into an adjacent shop, but neither has been available and won't be for years. I think I'll be able to open a second location in a couple of years, especially now that I have the specialty-cake side business going strong. I just have to be patient."

"I have no doubt you'll achieve your goals and dreams, Cassidy. You've been focused and driven since I met you fifteen years ago. You'll make it happen."

Warmth spread through her. As a bigwig for the

most successful company in town, let alone the county, Brandon's praise meant a lot to her.

His phone pinged and he took it from his pocket and glanced at it. "I didn't think today could get any better, but it actually has. The one and only Geoff Burris, rodeo champion, just texted that he's a yes to promote Taylor Beef. My dad's going to be ecstatic."

"Great news!" she said. "Congratulations." She raised her glass of orange juice to him, and he clinked it with his own. She thought of her friend Susanna trying to get through to Geoff Burris's team. It would a disappointment for Abernathy Meats, for sure.

He took her hand and held it, then took a bite of his French toast with the other. She recalled that he'd do this when they were in high school. They'd go to a pizza place and he'd hold her hand and eat a slice of pizza with the other. She used to think it was the most romantic thing. Kind of still was.

Three and a half hours later, when they'd returned from the second day of their parenting class and were checking out of the inn, Cassidy could hardly believe what a magical experience this had been.

And she had Winona Cobbs to thank. While Brandon was settling up at the desk, Cassidy stepped outside and looked up the telephone number for Wisdom by Winona. She pressed in the numbers and waited, hoping Winona would answer.

"Hello, Miss Ware."

"Goodness, you are psychic! Though I have proof of that already."

"Well, I also have caller ID," Winona deadpanned.

Cassidy felt her cheeks burn. "Ah, right. Well, I'm calling because Brandon Taylor and I are just leaving Lewistown now—we attended the parenting class on your advice and stayed at the lovely Blossom B and B, and the trip was just wonderful on every level."

"No surprise there," Winona said.

Cassidy grinned. "It was for me. I'd like to make an appointment with you for a reading."

"Delightful. You can pay me in a fancy coffee drink and two kinds of Danish, one for the road. I'll be at Bronco Java and Juice on Monday morning at six thirty. We'll chat there."

"Oh! Well, that sounds fine. I'll see you then."

"Yes, you will," Winona said before disconnecting.

"Checking in at the shop?" Brandon asked as he stepped out into the breezy sunshine with their bags.

"Actually, I just made an appointment with Winona Cobbs. She gave you this trip and it turned out to be everything we needed. Who knows what she'll tell me?"

He smiled. "She sure doesn't say much, but then much *happens*. And you know, I just realized she didn't charge me a cent. I usually get the Taylor name upcharge for everything."

"She's charging *me* a fancy coffee drink and two Danishes, one for the road."

"She could charge folks big bucks. Turns out my reading was priceless."

Cassidy leaned up and kissed him on the lips. "Agreed."

Barely an hour later, Brandon reluctantly pulled into a spot in front of Java and Juice, not ready to say goodbye to Cassidy, even for a few hours this afternoon. He zipped around to the passenger side and opened her door for her.

"I may never get used to that," she said.

"Sorry, you'll have to. It's the Taylor way. The pregnancy makes me doubly chivalrous." He got her suitcase from the cargo area and they headed upstairs.

Cassidy unlocked the door and they stepped inside. She slipped her arms around his neck. "Thank you for an incredible couple of days. Who knew taking a parenting class could be so life-changing? Plus, I can now properly swaddle an infant. Well, a doll."

He grinned and kissed her on the lips. "Winona Cobbs knew."

"I'm so excited for my reading on Monday morning. I'll let you know what she says."

He kissed her again. "Oh, you think you won't see me before Monday? I can't wait that long."

"Good. Want to come over tonight? We can cook or order in, watch a movie or bad reality TV."

"I'll see you at seven thirty," he said.

One more kiss—a long, hot one—and he was out the door. So far, being in a real relationship wasn't the straitjacket he'd thought it would be. He had no idea why, but he was grateful. He could give Cassidy what she needed and not feel the walls closing in on him. Win-win. He wasn't going to think about it; he'd just go with it.

He might have stayed a bit longer at Cassidy's, but he was itching to tell his dad the good news about Geoff Burris.

He found his father in his office, scanning and signing invoices.

"Dad, I told you I was confident that Geoff Burris would agree to star in our ad campaign, particularly ahead of the Mistletoe Rodeo in November," Brandon said, stopping in the doorway. "Mission accomplished."

He'd never seen his father get out of a chair so fast.

"Yes! Excellent." Cornelius pumped his fist in

the air—three times. "Jessica," he called at the top of his lungs. "Jessica!"

Brandon's stepmother came rushing in. "What on earth is all this yelling?"

"Brandon got Geoff Burris!" Cornelius exclaimed. "Taylor Beef will continue its reign over Abernathy Meats!" He actually did a little dance where he turned in a circle then grabbed Jessica into a dip.

"Great work, Brandon," his stepmother said with a grin. "Cornelius should be in a grand mood for a least three days." She chuckled, kissed her husband and then left the room.

"We'll have a small party to celebrate," Cornelius said. "Next Saturday night. Then we'll have our ad people get the word out to build excitement and we'll throw a big shindig at The Association."

"Sounds good, Dad." Brandon had no doubt his father would be in a good mood for weeks, not days.

"And the party will be just family," Cornelius added. "Your uncles, your siblings. Text them, will you?"

"Daphne is one of my siblings," Brandon said, staring at his father. Hard.

"Well, I did say siblings, didn't I? So yes, of course Daphne is invited."

Would wonders never cease. This good mood

of Cornelius's might last a *month*. Maybe even forever.

"Daphne is family even if I don't like how she's living her life," Cornelius said. He moved over to the bar against the wall and took down two glasses. "She can invite her fiancé, too."

Brandon extended his hand. "I'm proud of you, Dad. But it's about damned time."

His father scowled and waved his hand dismissively, but he was too happy for the frown to last. He reached for the Scotch, top label. "I didn't say I'd actually *talk* to Daphne, just that she was welcome to attend. Vegetarian lifestyle. Animal sanctuary. Who in their right mind ever heard of such a thing from an heir of a cattle ranching empire? I figure a family party celebrating a Taylor Beef score will make her see that family comes first, not personal nonsense."

Now that was more like Cornelius Taylor. Brandon shook his head, wishing he could actually get through to his father, but years of dealing with him had told him he wouldn't. The man was completely self-absorbed.

Brandon was about to rescind the *I'm proud of you*, but his father grabbed him into a bear hug.

"*I'm* so damned proud of *you*," Cornelius said. "Did the personal days you took have anything to do with winning over Burris?"

"Actually, no. I attended a two-day class with

someone special. And in fact, since this will be a family party, you can add one more to the guest list."

"You get married or something?" Cornelius asked, eyes narrowed on him. He looked like he was bracing himself for terrible news.

"No. But I'm going to be a father. Cassidy Ware is pregnant."

Cornelius's eyes practically popped out. "Am I supposed to congratulate you? I can't tell."

He felt like he'd just taken a left hook to the jaw. His father had to ask?

"Yes, Dad. Congratulations are in order. Cassidy and I are a couple and we're expecting."

Cornelius picked up the Scotches and handed him one. "A new generation of Taylor Beef heirs! Brandon, that's wonderful. Today just keeps getting better."

Hadn't Brandon just thought that earlier about his own day?

"You're happy about having a grandchild or happy that you're getting a baby heir?" Brandon asked.

"They're one and the same, son. I couldn't be more thrilled."

So Cornelius Taylor. "I expect you to babysit, Dad," Brandon said with a smile.

"With Jessica's help, sure. Where's my cell phone?" he asked, looking at his desk and the credenza and the bar. "Who can ever find that thing? I have some gloating calls to make around town. A new generation of heirs! That is something else. Well done, Brandon. Well done, indeed."

Good Lord. He really hadn't known how his father would take the news. Part of him had expected Cornelius to erupt with rage over losing another son to a personal life—and this time a baby. His dad might be 100 percent focused on the word *heir*, but maybe deep down where he barely knew his father, the man was actually happy about being a granddad.

"Hold off on making any calls, Dad. Cassidy's very newly pregnant. I'll let you know when you can call everyone you know."

"Fine, fine," Cornelius said. "You get in touch with your sister about the party. We'll have it here at the ranch. Oh, and I'll call that nice architect back and set up a meeting for you. She can design you a grand house right here on the ranch with a nursery."

Cornelius took that moment to raise his glass in a toast.

Brandon kept his glass down. "I'm not sure of my plans, Dad. Or what Cassidy wants." Now that they were a couple, getting married was definitely off the table. He had to ease into being in a real relationship. A platonic marriage—no problem. A real marriage? A shiver ran up Brandon's spine.

Cornelius scowled, but again, he was too happy about his heir-to-be that it didn't last long. The mirth was back in his eyes. "Well, you bring Cassidy to the party."

Brandon clinked to that.

Chapter Twelve

A potbellied pig named Tiny Tim was sniffing his cowboy boot. Brandon had wanted to stop by Happy Hearts, his sister's animal sanctuary, this afternoon before he got bogged down in a few hours of work. Daphne, in overalls and muck boots, was feeding the pig and a surly-looking goat in their pens. Tiny Tim's snout was more interested in Brandon's boot than in his breakfast.

"Aw, he likes you," Daphne said, pushing her long strawberry-blond ponytail behind her shoulder. "So you said you had some very interesting news for me. I'm all ears."

He explained about Geoff Burris. And their father's invitation.

"So he envisions my attendance as an opportunity to reprogram me, is that it?" She rolled her eyes good-naturedly and shook her head. "Dad will never change, will he?"

"Nope," Brandon said. "Think you'll come?"

"To spend time with the whole family, yes, I absolutely will. Having Evan by my side, even figuratively, will give me strength to deal with Dad. To be completely ignored by Dad, I should say."

Brandon grinned. "I'm glad you'll be there."

"So how are things with you and Cassidy?" she asked, adding what looked like kale and spinach to Tiny Tim's huge food bowl.

"I found out what she needed," Brandon said. "And came through."

Daphne's blue eyes lit up. "Yeah? Can I ask? I'm dying to know."

"She needs us to be a couple, a real couple. She needs me to try to give it my all. So that's what I'm doing."

"Brandon, that's great. Good for both of you."

"Not necessarily good for the baby," he said on a sulky note.

"What? How could it not be? The baby's parents are in a committed relationship."

"And if it doesn't work out? If Cassidy and I just piss each other off after this honeymoon phase and suddenly we're fighting and break up? Then we're both all bitter and arguing over who gets the baby what days."

Daphne turned to look at him. "Why get so ahead of yourself—and to a place that you very likely won't go?"

"How can you know, though? Not one relationship of mine has worked out. Why would this one?"

"Because of how you feel about Cassidy," Daphne said. "Plain and simple. And I'll tell you, Brandon. I don't even think how you feel about her is connected to her being pregnant. I mean, it's powerful stuff—she's going to be the mother of your child. But your feelings for Cassidy are because of *her*."

"How could you possibly know that?" he asked, reaching down to touch Tiny Tim's soft ear. He got a snort of thanks before the pig went back to eating.

"I could tell from the way you were talking about her the day you told me she was pregnant. You feel about Cassidy the way I feel about Evan. When someone is that right for you, it's obvious. It's also out of your control."

He frowned. "I like to be in control of myself."

Daphne chuckled. "Love is big stuff. Just let it do its thing. Stop trying to mess with it."

"I never said anything about love. Cassidy and I are in a relationship, a romantic relationship. Stop putting words in my mouth."

Daphne laughed again. "Poor Brandon. Madly in love and fighting like hell against it."

"Those are more words, Daphne."

Luckily, her phone rang and she had to get over to the adoptable animals barn. He couldn't take much more of his sister right now.

Madly in love. He and Cassidy were testing things out. No one said anything about love.

He and Cassidy were about *need*. She needed real romance out of him. He needed—

Brandon froze, realizing that what he needed was at odds with what she'd gotten from him.

He needed a platonic marriage so that they could raise their child in peace and harmony. But instead, she would be leading him to a real marriage—the natural progression from a real relationship.

For a smart guy, he sure was stupid sometimes. She'd all but spelled it out, that for their baby's sake, they should try the real thing. What the hell had he thought she'd meant? He shook his head.

Calm the hell down, he told himself. *Just go slow.*

"Later, Tiny Tim," he told the potbellied pig and stalked toward his truck.

He got in, his shoulders bunched, his head out of sorts. A drive would do him good.

Distracted, he ended up turning onto a road that would lead him right into Bronco Valley, the area of town where Cassidy had grown up. He remembered where she lived: 401 Elm Street.

He didn't spend much time in the Valley since his life was focused in the Heights. And now that he thought about it, he didn't have any friends in this part of Bronco, either. But he had no doubt that many employees of the Taylor Ranch lived in the Valley, and the Taylor family should be more involved in the community than it was. Fancy fundraisers were one thing. Real involvement, doing the work itself, was another. Taylor Beef was deeply involved in investing in ranching communities, but Bronco wasn't all ranches.

He found the house by memory, almost surprised it came back to him. The peeling, faded yellow one-story home was the same boxlike structure, with a chain-link fence on one side. He parked across the street and stared at the uninviting residence, having a hard time imagining Cassidy, as a young girl or a teenager, finding inspiration walking that uneven path and up the broken steps—the top one, raised on the left side, had a dangerous gash in the concrete—and going inside. Then again, she must have, given how driven she was. She'd wanted to have her own business since she was a preteen. She'd seen it as a way out, something that was hers.

A young couple with a toddler wearing a pink wool hat with bear ears came out of the house. The woman, her long dark hair in a ponytail, was singing a song about a meatball rolling off a table and out the door, and the toddler joined in when she knew a word, making the man with them laugh. They looked happy. Very happy.

You didn't need money to be happy, Brandon knew. He had too much money and he hadn't been happy for a long time—until Cassidy had come back into his life.

But then the man tripped on the uneven step and almost fell, and the little girl screamed, "Daddy!"

Brandon grimaced, got out of his car and held up a hand. "You okay?"

"I'm fine," the guy said. "Do it every day even though I know it's there." He shook his head on a chuckle.

The woman smiled. "You always forget to step over that part of the step where it's split. Amanda and I always remember, right, honey bunny?"

"Right!" the little girl said. She looked up at Brandon. "I'm two." She held up two fingers.

Brandon grinned at her. "I like your hat," he told her. He turned toward the couple. "I know the family that used to live here. Do you own this house now?"

"Yeah," the man said. "Bought it five years ago and meant to fix it up, but times are tough."

Brandon looked at the steps. Were they like that when Cassidy lived there? He couldn't remember.

The couple of times he'd dropped Cassidy off here, he did recall staring at the house and being confused that anyone could live in a tiny box like this. Rich privilege, he thought, shaking his head. And snotty and wrong. People did the best they could with what they had.

Brandon looked at the couple. "As I said, I know the family that lived here and, in their honor, I'd like to send out a mason to take care of these steps. No charge to you whatsoever."

They stared at each other then turned to Brandon.

"You're serious?" the man asked. "What's the catch?"

"No catch. Just in memory of the woman who owned the house. She was a single mother and raised one heck of a daughter. Now you're raising a daughter here. I'd just like to do something in her memory."

"That's really nice," the woman said. "No strings?"

"No strings."

"Thank you," the man said. "We'll definitely take you up on that. The people that lived here, we didn't meet them, but they must have been good folks if you care that much about them."

Brandon extended a hand and both shook it. "The steps will be repaired this week. Take care."

As he walked back to his truck, he wasn't sure if he'd mention this to Cassidy. It seemed like something that was between him and her mother, who he'd never gotten to meet because she'd been at work the couple of times he'd been over. Or maybe it was just between him and his conscience—for not doing more to build up Bronco Valley. He'd talk to his brother Jordan about forming a revitalization company; he had no doubt the entire family would get involved.

As he headed back to Bronco Heights, he thought about her mother's sacrifices, her dreams for her daughter, her support of Cassidy. And Cassidy's own dreams, her goals. An idea fixed in his head and the more he thought it over, the more right it felt. He wouldn't tell Cassidy about this, either. He'd let it be a surprise.

With that idea taking center stage in his brain, he was thankfully distracted from his conversation with his sister, which now seemed like yesterday. He made a call, then a stop in town, then drove to the Taylor Ranch, ready to get back to work. Because he'd spend most of it anticipating tonight with Cassidy.

Then again, maybe he should cancel. Given his frame of mind, he'd be on the quiet side and she'd know something was wrong. And something *was* wrong.

But he wanted to see her, *had* to see her, even if their very real relationship was causing his chest to tighten on him.

* * *

"Something smells amazing," Brandon said, sniffing the air as he stepped through the door of Cassidy's apartment.

She kissed him on the lips and then closed it behind him. "I'm making a stir-fry and it's almost done. Go make yourself comfortable. You can root through the TV for a movie or show. I love how domestic all this is," she called in a happy voice from the kitchen.

Domestic. He'd never really liked that word. He dropped down on the sofa, aiming the cable remote at the television on the wooden stand. He scrolled through the channel guide—movies, reality shows, documentaries, romantic comedies. Nothing caught his eye. He shifted on the sofa, crossing a foot over his knee. Uncrossing. Trying to get comfortable. The back of his neck itched. Now his shoulders felt tight. Bunched.

Weird. What the hell was wrong with him?

I love how domestic this is...

He stood up, shutting off the TV. Something was bugging him.

Suddenly, the smell of the stir-fry seemed cloying more than anything. This whole set-up seemed kind of...homey. Marriage-y. The kind of thing married people did. Domestic.

When they'd originally made these plans, he hadn't realized *how* domestic it all was. A home-cooked meal. Watching TV. Sharing popcorn on the couch and talking about their days. When was the last time he'd done that with a woman? Brandon and his dates always went out to fine restaurants. And if they went back to the woman's place, it wasn't to watch a romantic comedy while snuggling on the sofa.

He stared at her sofa and it suddenly seemed like the gateway to walking down the aisle in a tuxedo, his bow tie strangling him. He didn't want to get married. He didn't want this beautiful thing with Cassidy to turn bitter and ugly. He had to protect his relationship with his child.

Okay, calm down, buddy. You're having some kind of confirmed bachelor panic attack.

Cassidy used the words *try us out* and *give us a chance*, he reminded himself. She hadn't been talking about marriage.

But that's what she wants. That's where this is all leading.

He dropped back onto the sofa, half expecting ropes to come darting out of the cushions to trap him forever.

"Dinner's ready!" Cassidy called.

He slowly got up. No ropes pulled him back.

He had to be losing his mind. What the hell was going on with him? His head and heart and mind and body seemed to be at war, each yanking him in a different direction.

Poor Brandon, he heard his sister say in his head. *Madly in love and fighting like hell against it.*

No. Once again, he'd never said anything about love. This was a trial romance. Feeling each other out to see if they were good together. It wasn't going to last. He'd known that when he'd agreed to give it a shot. He'd tried and now he was quickly discovering that he wasn't cut out for a real relationship. No surprise there.

He also knew he'd have to get out before things got too out of hand. Maybe he should tell Cassidy tonight that he thought they should go back to the way things were before Lewistown. Platonic partners in pregnancy and child-rearing. He could make a stronger case for marriage now that they'd tried this real relationship thing and it wasn't working out. For *him*, anyway. Cassidy seemed fine with it.

She was happy.

Very happy.

And he was going destroy that? *Um, Cassidy, we have to break up because this isn't what I want and it's messing with me. Love doesn't last. Marriage doesn't last. Let's just get out of this now and save our friendship. For the baby's sake.*

He told himself to wait for a pause in their conversation and go from there.

He stepped into the kitchen, hoping his expression didn't match the turmoil inside his head. Cassidy was bringing two plates of steaming stir-fry to the table. A bouquet of flowers was in the center of that table, and he realized he hadn't brought them.

"I should have brought you flowers," he said. "I got caught up in conversation with my dad and then my sister, and my head exploded."

That was an in. Of sorts.

"Yikes, what was the gist?" she asked, sitting.

He sat, as well, and explained about the celebration party and how Cornelius had only invited Daphne to reprogram her into someone she wasn't and would never be.

"Why isn't it enough to be his daughter?" Brandon asked. "Why must she be a meat-eater? Why can't she protect animals? Why can't she just be who she is?"

"I agree," Cassidy said.

"People should be allowed to be who they are, not who others want them to be." Yes. That was true. He was who he was. Cassidy was trying to turn him into a TV husband and father.

No. *She's not trying to do anything but be who she is*, he corrected. *Leave her alone*.

Losing. His. Mind.

"You know what?" he said. "Let's change the subject to something that has nothing to do with my father."

He couldn't say a word about the rest of the conversation with Daphne. About them. Him. And how uneasy he'd felt in the Happy Hearts' barn, being accused of *loving* Cassidy.

She took a bite of her stir-fry, then popped up and grabbed a magazine off the counter. "How's this for a change of subject? A parenting quiz in *Baby* magazine."

He ate a bite of the chicken and vegetables and rice, which was delicious and did not turn to sludge in his stomach. The change of subject had helped already. "With all the reading I've done and the two-day class, I should ace this."

She smiled. "Me, too." She quickly ate another bite of stir-fry. "Okay, first question. 'Your newborn is crying inconsolably. You rock her, you feed her, you change her. Still crying her eyes out. You…(A) Call her pediatrician and ask for advice, even if it's midnight. Every doctor has an after-hours service. (B) Let her cry. She has to learn to self-soothe! (C) You're too busy crying yourself from frustration at how hard parenthood is to help your newborn.'"

"Um, the last one?" he said. "Kidding. Although I can see that happening. I'm going to say A. According to my fatherhood book and Paul Woodsley, newborns shouldn't be left to cry and self-soothe because they're too young for that."

Cassidy grinned. "Correct! Now you ask me the next one."

He slid the magazine over. "'Your baby is ten

months old. You've never left him with a sitter because, to be honest, it makes you a little nervous. You now have two tickets—great seats!—to your dream event. You…(A) Get over yourself and ask the teenager next door if she can sit for you. (B) Give the tickets away. (C) Call a trusted sitter from the list you've been adding to since the baby was born, developed from friends and family and neighbors—'

"Wait," he said, looking at Cassidy. "People go ten months without leaving their homes?"

She laughed. "I'm sure some do. I can imagine being a very protective parent, not wanting to leave my baby with a stranger. If none of my friends are available and I desperately need a sitter, I'd probably cancel on the event. I sure wouldn't choose A, desperately asking sullen teen Sarah Peterman from the Blossom B and B!"

"I'd watch the baby for you," he said.

She reached across and squeezed his hand. "And I for you." She took a sip of her water. "But hopefully we'd be attending the events *together*. I'm gonna go with C. The one with the trusted list."

"Correct," he said. "Though think about all the events I'll be able to get *out of* once the baby is born. Dreaded fundraisers. I'm fine with writing the check. It's the small talk that kills me."

"I've always liked small talk. Nice and light conversation. I chat with people in line at the grocery store, while waiting to get my car inspected, with the mail carrier, you name it."

"Weirdo," he said with a smile. "A weirdo who makes great chicken stir-fry."

She laughed. "Did you find a movie for us to watch?"

Such a normal, easy question. Much easier than any of those in the parenting quiz. And yet it made his throat close up to the point he had to put his fork down.

The craziest thing was that he *wanted* to be sitting there with Cassidy, having this home-cooked meal and taking parenting quizzes and then watching a romantic comedy or thriller. It was just the concept itself that made the walls of this tiny apartment feel like they were closing in. How did that make sense?

Hell, maybe Daphne was right. Maybe he was fighting against his feelings for Cassidy. He clearly was.

Why had he talked to his father earlier? Why had he gone to Daphne's? The key to him being okay with a real relationship with Cassidy was being completely out of his own life, away from memories—past and present—that reinforced how he felt. Love and marriage didn't last. People got hurt. One of his uncles always said, "Start as you mean to continue," and Brandon thought that was a great saying, important advice. If he didn't get emotionally involved, no one would get hurt. He and Cassidy could have a terrific platonic relationship, and their child would be raised happily. No yelling parents. No *You said. You promised. Why didn't you. I hate you.* None of that.

Watching a movie would just make things worse. He'd be too in his own head, overthinking, getting way ahead of himself. What he needed was to distract himself. To lose himself. He needed Lewistown in Cassidy's tiny apartment.

"I have a better idea," he said. "Let's make our own unfilmed love scene in your bedroom."

That brought a giggle out of her and a slight blush to her cheeks. "Sounds good to me. Best movie possible."

"Right?" he asked, reaching for her hand and kissing it. *I just don't want to hurt you. I'd hate myself forever.*

As they finished dinner, he felt better. He could sway things, as he'd just done, to make domesticity in a real relationship bearable. Maybe that would help. But for how long?

Once in the bedroom, Brandon forgot all about being claustrophobic and commitment-phobic. Cassidy was like a dream come true in bed, much better than his fantasies had ever been. They fit together so well, in perfect rhythm, in total sync.

When the alarm on the bedside table went off

at 5:00 a.m. the next morning, his eyes were already open, the walls once again moving in. He just needed a little time to regroup, to think. He'd go riding, get his bearings, figure out what he was going to do. He had to tread very carefully.

As she stirred in bed and then sat up, he quickly dressed, turned down her kind offer to come down to the shop for coffee and breakfast, and for a moment, just admired how beautiful Cassidy looked all sleepy-eyed, her blond hair a little wild. He kissed her goodbye, his head a jumble.

As she walked him to the door, he realized he'd never mentioned that she was invited to the family party. "I completely forgot to mention this last night. That party my dad's throwing? He personally invited you because you're now family. He's the only one besides Daphne who knows about the pregnancy. We can tell my brothers and uncles at the party Saturday night."

She stared at him. "You completely forgot to mention this? How?"

"I had a lot on my mind last night. The talk with my dad was weird. Then I went to Daphne's and that got weird, too. Then the day went unexpected places and by the time I arrived here, I was tied in knots, I guess. And once we were in bed, I forgot *everything*." He tried to smile, but it must have come out awkwardly. He sighed inwardly, hating what he was doing. Hating how unsettled and off balance he was. How damned uncomfortable. With the only woman he'd ever been completely himself with. Hell, maybe that was a lot of the problem here.

"You okay, Brandon?" she asked, studying him.

Not really. I don't know what I'm doing. I want to be with you. But it feels wrong, like we're on a kiddie roller coaster that's about turn wild and crash.

How did he explain all that?

"You did seem kind of distant last night," Cassidy said. "Same thing this morning. You can talk to me, you know."

"I know." He made a show of looking at his phone for the time. "I have to go. Early-morning video-conference call. Have a good day."

"You, too," she said…hesitantly.

The last thing he wanted was to make her feel insecure. He *was* being distant and he knew it.

But I don't want to talk about it until I work it out for myself. I want to give this a bit more time. I'm not ready to tell her it's not working for me.

If he did tell her he wanted to go back to the way things were before Lewistown, who knew what she'd do? Maybe she'd be brokenhearted and he'd feel like the pits of hell. Maybe she'd be furious and tell him she'd see him in court to discuss custody issues. A cold blast ran up his spine.

He really needed some wisdom from Winona Cobbs, but the elderly woman would just give him some cryptic two-liner and send him on his way.

He was going to have to figure this out for himself.

Chapter Thirteen

Cassidy practically flew down the steps to Java and Juice at five thirty on Monday morning. She wanted to make sure the bulk of her baking was done by the time Winona Cobbs would arrive at six thirty for her reading.

And especially given the new direction of her relationship with Brandon—and the awkwardness between them Friday night and Saturday morning—Cassidy wanted to hear that all would be well. Plus, she was dying to know what Winona had meant the other day. *You'll be glad you did it.*

Glad she did *what*? Told Brandon what she needed? What else had she done lately?

As she let herself in the back door, she wondered if Brandon was already regretting agreeing to a committed relationship. She'd gotten to know him so well that when he'd come over on Friday night and was a little quieter than usual, she'd taken it as him distancing himself. Sure, maybe he had been preoccupied with whatever had gone on with his father, then Daphne, and the rest of the afternoon, which he'd mentioned had been heavy.

But forgetting to mention that she was invited to his family party until he was about to leave the next morning? That was telling. Did he not want her there? Did putting her and family in the same sentence make him uncomfortable? Was it too much too soon?

Something was bothering him. Maybe being home, back on his own turf, had him feeling uneasy about being in a real relationship, opening himself up to risk. The magic of getting away for two days was one thing, but being home, business as usual, might have gotten its grips on him. He hadn't suggested getting together Saturday night, and though she'd picked up her phone ten times to text him to come over and talk, she wanted to give him some breathing room.

He'd texted twice on Sunday, a meme that had made her laugh and a link to an article on what type of music babies in the womb should listen to—all kinds. His getting in touch had made her feel better, and she'd had a busy bunch of hours at Java and Juice, then had spent the rest of the afternoon working on an expansion plan for the business. She'd had a brainstorm of opening up another location in Lewistown, where she'd made so many happy memories. The bustling town would be perfect. She couldn't put the ole cart before the horse, though; she'd make an appointment with her bank and, if she got approved for a loan based on her business plan, she'd go scout out locations.

Incredible, she thought. Not too long ago, she was moping around a barn on her thirtieth birthday. Now she was in love. Going to be a mother. And possibly have her business dreams realized. She had to stop worrying about Brandon. If they weren't okay, he'd tell her. Brandon was honest and forthright. And anyway, Winona Cobbs would set her straight very soon.

The next hour went by too slowly, even though Cassidy was super busy, making muffins and scones and her special English muffins for the breakfast sandwiches that Hank and Helen would cook up. Finally, dozens of baked goods out of the oven and in the display case, a knock came at the back door.

Cassidy dashed over. Winona stood there, wearing a purple turban, a long purple sweater, and silver-colored leggings. She also wore purple cowboy boots. Cassidy loved the way Winona dressed. Ninety-four and full of style.

"Morning, Winona," she said. "I've got your Danishes waiting for you. What's your coffee order?" she asked, heading back to the counter.

"I'd like something fun instead of the boring old regular coffee I always have at home. Maybe something with caramel. You pick."

"I've got just the drink for you," Cassidy said. "A caramel macchiato. Vanilla syrup, steamed milk, espresso and a drizzle of caramel syrup. So comforting and delicious."

Winona winked. "I'll take it."

Cassidy made the drink and plated a Danish, bagging up one more as promised in case it slipped her mind later. "Here you are."

"Let's talk in the kitchen," Winona said. "I know you have some cleanup to do."

"Right you are."

Winona eyed her. "I know."

Cassidy smiled and led the way into the kitchen. She started cleaning up bits of dough and powdered sugar and icing. "First, I'd like to ask you what you meant by 'You'll be glad you did it.'"

"You haven't done it yet," Winona said. "Let's just leave it at that."

Cassidy brightened. "Oh. Well, since I'll be glad, that's fine, then."

"Yes, it is." Winona sat in the chair Helen always used when she needed a break from standing. "Here's what I have to tell you, Miss Ware. You are not the captain of your own ship—not anymore."

Cassidy frowned. "But my mother loved that saying. She always told me that I *was* the captain of my own ship."

"You used to be. But not anymore. You have a co-captain now."

"Oh! Of course, you mean Brandon."

"Yes, I mean Brandon." Winona sipped her drink. "My, is this good. So rich and decadent. I just love it."

Cassidy smiled. "I'm glad."

Winona took a bite of her Danish. "Delicious. Absolutely delicious." She stood and put the rest of the Danish into the bag with the other one, then took another sip of her coffee. "Have a lovely day, dear."

Cassidy stared at her. "Wait. What about my reading?"

Winona tilted her head. "Weren't you listening?"

"I'm not the captain of my own ship, not anymore?" Cassidy asked, trying to not sound too disappointed. That was her *entire* reading?

Winona adjusted her turban. "Exactly."

With that, Winona took her bag of Danishes and left by the back door.

Humph.

Cassidy glanced at the clock. Six forty-five. That

meant her appointment had lasted all of fifteen minutes. And half that time was spent making the caramel macchiato!

She couldn't think too much more about it because Helen and Hank arrived, and then a lot of customers, helping Cassidy's mood by ordering a lot of pricey drinks and smoothies.

"Hi, Cassidy!"

She turned to find Sofia Sanchez coming up to the counter. A beautiful young woman, Sofia's usually straight long red hair was styled in beachy waves past her shoulders, her dark brown eyes on the beautiful red coat hanging on a hook by the aprons. Sofia was a stylist at BH Couture, where Brandon had bought the coat.

"I love that coat so much," Sofia said with a grin. "It's one of my favorites at BH Couture."

Cassidy grinned back. "And I hear I have you to thank. I'm a little mortified to know you caught me staring all dreamily at the coat for weeks to confirm it for Brandon."

"Are you kidding? What do you think I do all day at work? Stare at items totally out of my price range, even with my employee discount."

Cassidy laughed. "Well, thank you. I love it."

"I have to say, I never thought Brandon Taylor would settle down. We only went out a couple times before he told me he'd just like to be friends. But I got the sense immediately that he was the ultimate confirmed bachelor. That no woman would ever win his heart to get him down the aisle."

Had Cassidy won his heart? She really wasn't sure. Sometimes she thought so, based on how he looked at her, how he acted. Then sometimes, like Friday night and Saturday morning… "Sofia, what do you mean you never thought he would settle down?" Sofia must think he *had* settled down. Because of the coat?

"Oh, it's clear you're the one," Sofia said. "Just like my sister Camilla was the one for the *former* Most Eligible Bachelor in Bronco—he-who-supposedly-wouldn't-be-tamed Jordan Taylor. Seems like when Taylor men finally fall, they fall hard and that's that." She glanced at the coat. "Oh yes. He fell hard."

Cassidy glanced at the coat also. "Men have been buying women expensive gifts since the dawn of time. Hard to read anything into that."

"Yeah, but I saw the look in his eyes and heard the emotion in his voice when he was double-checking about the coat. Love knocks a man upside the head. For a while there, he's all disoriented. Then he comes to and fully wakes up. Brandon strikes me as someone who's been trying to control his single status for years. But no one can control how they feel deep down. Not Jordan Taylor and not Brandon."

"Thank you," Cassidy whispered. "I might have

needed to hear that right now. Any coffee drink or smoothie on the house."

"Oooh, I'll take a berry explosion smoothie," Sofia said.

As Cassidy made the drink, she couldn't help but wonder what Sofia's love life was like. Given the personal conversation they'd just had about Cassidy, she could probably ask. But she didn't want to pry since Sofia hadn't brought it up herself.

A few minutes later, when Cassidy handed over her drink and then watched her walk away, she was amazed at how full of surprises life really was. At Jordan and Camilla's wedding, Cassidy had been a little jealous of Sofia, especially when she and Brandon had been talking so close. And now, Sofia was the one who'd lifted Cassidy's spirits.

Her phone pinged with a text, a much-needed interruption from her thoughts. Except the text was from Brandon.

How'd the reading go?

Cassidy bit her lip and texted her reply.

Not sure. She told me I wasn't the captain of my own ship anymore, that I had a co-captain.

Am I the co-captain or is the baby?

Cassidy hadn't even considered the baby in that equation.

You are—I confirmed. Winona left after fifteen minutes.

Yeah, she shooed me out after fifteen minutes, too.

Winona wasn't much of a talker. But what she did say ran deep. It was up to Cassidy to figure out what Winona had meant. If she could.

I was hoping for something a little more substantial.

I'd give it time. Winona's wisdom works in mysterious ways.

Cassidy smiled. She sent a smiley cowboy emoticon and Brandon texted back a thumbs-up.

But after Friday night and Saturday morning, she was just slightly worried about what was going on with Brandon. Maybe she didn't want to know anything else.

Woof! Woof, woof!

Maggie? Cassidy rushed to the back door, and there she was. The brown-and-white Australian shepherd. This could very well be Maggie, escapee from Happy Hearts. She couldn't let the dog in the shop, so she went outside to pet her while she called Daphne Taylor.

"Oh my gosh! I'm on my way!" Daphne said.

Cassidy texted her part-time employee to cover the counter while she dashed in to get the leash hanging from the hook, leaving the door slightly open so she could soothingly talk to the dog. "You can't run away this time. Don't you want your forever home? If you're not Maggie, I'll bet Daphne will take you in and find you a home. Don't you want to go where you truly belong?"

Woof! the dog responded.

"You are such a good dog." Cassidy carefully slipped the leash around Maggie's neck, trying to attach the clasp to the corded part, but Maggie gave a woof and slipped out of the makeshift collar. She took off, leaving Cassidy with an empty leash.

Noooo!

"Pup, come back!"

Cassidy went racing down the little alley, looking in every direction for the dog, but she didn't see her. She caught her breath then called Daphne again.

"I'm so sorry," Cassidy said. "The dog got away while I was trying to attach the leash I bought."

"Oh darn." Daphne sighed. "We'll get her eventually. Thanks for trying, Cassidy. Oh, and I'll see you Saturday where I can properly congratulate you."

Cassidy beamed. "I'm excited about meeting the Taylors. And by the way, what's the dress code? Should I dress up?"

"Family party at the ranch? Let's see…my father will be in his crispest jeans, a Western shirt and one of his hundreds of Stetsons. Jessica, my stepmother, will be in a shift dress with a tiny cardigan over her shoulders and high heels. I'll be in a Happy Hearts T-shirt."

Cassidy almost gasped. Based on what Brandon had told her, their father would go nuts. "Really?"

Daphne laughed. "No way. Totally joking. I'll wear a casual dress."

"A casual dress—perfect. I appreciate the help. I'm really sorry about Maggie."

"We'll find her. See you soon."

The chat with Daphne made her feel a little more connected to the Taylor family. The last time she'd gone to a Taylor function was Jordan's wedding, and she'd been part of the catering team. Now she was going to be a guest at a family party. Her baby *was* a Taylor.

Suddenly she did want to know her future, what was going to be. Were she and Brandon going to work out just fine, get married, live happily-ever-after?

If she had a Magic 8-Ball, she was pretty sure it would tell her to ask again later.

Chapter Fourteen

On Tuesday morning, Cassidy was surprised to look up from the cash register in Java and Juice to find Brandon next in line. He was in business casual, which meant he was working from home at the cattle ranch instead of the Taylor Beef offices in town. Dark jeans, long-sleeved button-down shirt, and cowboy boots. Could he be any sexier?

"Hey, beautiful."

She most definitely did not look beautiful. She was tired, had powdered sugar in her hair, and her apron was covered with icing from a doughnut a toddler pressed against her "to see if it would stick." Her face *had* to register the crazy morning, and the shop had only been open for a little over an hour. "Hi, yourself." Her face also had to register how good it was to see him.

"I mentioned to my stepmother that I was headed into town and she asked me to pick up four quarts of juice. She said the same as her last order."

Ah, Jessica Taylor and her quarts of juice. Cassidy loved that. It was like having twenty customers in one. "Ah, I can easily call it up." Cassidy typed "Taylor" into her tablet and Jessica's last order appeared. Half were green juices and half were fruit.

"I wish I could see you tonight," he said, "but I've got late meetings with our ad agency to go over concepts for the Burris ad campaign." He wasn't quite looking at her since he was reaching for his wallet. Brandon was different since Lewistown. Or the same as he'd been *before*.

Her heart went south. "Oh…well, another night then." She tried to keep the disappointment out of her voice. She knew Brandon was going through a "thing" and she had to let him work it out. He'd gone from "I will never be in a committed romantic relationship with strings again" to being in exactly that. She couldn't expect that he'd always find it comfortable. Still, she had an important appointment today that could result in good news and she'd been hoping they could celebrate if there was cause.

"Definitely," he said. But he didn't suggest a night.

"Brandon, I'm a straight shooter. Are we okay?" Nothing wrong with asking, she told herself. You didn't ask, you didn't find out. She'd kept it light and simple.

He gave her hand a squeeze. "We're okay. I've just got a lot on my plate. I will definitely see you Saturday night."

Saturday night? It was *Tuesday*.

They definitely were not okay.

"Text me if you need anything," he said and then left with his shopping bag of pricey juices for his stepmother.

At least he came in. If he were truly trying to avoid her, he would have made an excuse not to do Jessica the favor.

The shop got busy and didn't let up. As usual, Cassidy was grateful for the distraction. And then, finally, at two thirty, she took off her apron, speed-cleaned and was grateful her service was coming in for the weekly deep clean. Cassidy had to get ready for her appointment. The appointment of all appointments!

Butterflies let loose in her stomach. Today she was meeting with a loan officer at Bronco Bank and Trust about her goal to open a second location in Lewistown. She was confident she'd be approved. But not *too* confident. The bank could easily say no. That she was doing fine with one location but not fine enough to justify them giving her money for a second. Her business plan was sound, though. She'd added the revenue her side business had brought in and what she expected going forward. She had her papers in order. She even had testimonials from Bronco residents.

If she got the loan, she'd let Brandon know a celebration was in order, and they could have a magical night in Lewistown sometime this week, scouting locations for her second shop. When she'd opened the shop in Bronco Heights, she'd been alone, her mother freshly gone. Now she'd have Brandon by her side, sharing in her joy, her success.

If he didn't let his head start controlling his heart again.

Cassidy headed upstairs, showered and changed into a black pantsuit and her pumps, packing her business plan into a leather folder that her mother had bought her for her eighteenth birthday. *Dear Future Businesswoman, you'll need this*, her mother had written on the card. She hugged it against her chest. "I'm gonna make you proud, Mom," she said heavenward.

At four o'clock, Cassidy sat across from David Harwood, loan officer. Despite her being prepared in every way, the man was intimidating because of his title. He held her future in his hands.

No, she corrected. *He doesn't. You do. You've got this.*

She took out her business plan and was about to begin her well-rehearsed speech when Harwood held up a hand.

"No need to convince me," he said. "You're approved for a half million dollars. I've drawn up the paperwork, so if you'll just sign here." He slid the paperwork across the desk.

"Wait, *what*?" she said. "Approved for five hundred thousand dollars? I didn't ask for even *half* that much in my online application."

"A benefactor has backed you, Miss Ware," he said. "Brandon Taylor. You're all set."

The air whooshed out of her and she sat back, stunned.

And angry.

What. The. Hell.

"I don't understand," she said. "When did he do this?" Brandon didn't know she was coming here today.

"Mr. Taylor called the owner of the bank personally this past Friday afternoon to discuss it, then came in just before closing to sign the necessary documents to transfer funds on an as-requested basis by you."

Good Lord. The day they'd gotten back from Lewistown. She remembered they'd talked about her hopes of expanding. She'd mentioned it was still a "someday" goal financially speaking.

She slid the paperwork back across the desk. "I filled out an online application. And I have a solid business plan typed up. I'd like you to consider me on my own merits."

The loan officer's mouth dropped open. "Are you saying you don't want the preapproved funding?"

"Yes, that is exactly what I'm saying. Mr. Harwood, please consider my application and read over my business plan. I've worked hard to build Bronco Java and Juice into a successful shop and I know a second location in a town with a much larger population will be even more successful."

He accepted her leather folder. "I'll be in touch," he said and shook her hand.

With that, she stood and walked away, fury mingling with embarrassment. Cassidy had never been one to care what anyone thought. But did the entire bank think her boyfriend was bankrolling her?

She stalked back to the shop and got in her car. She was about to tell Brandon Taylor what he could do with his half million dollars.

Cassidy had been to the Taylor Ranch twice before, once when Camilla Sanchez had first hired her to cater drinks and desserts for her wedding and had showed her where she'd set up, and then for the wedding itself. She drove up the winding road toward the main house, just able to catch a glimpse of the stables through the trees. How different would her life be at this moment if she hadn't escaped to see the horses that night? Or if she'd gone back to the wedding before Brandon had arrived at the stables?

One thing she knew was that she would have still gone to the bank with her business plan, full speed ahead on her goals and dreams. She parked and bit her lip, actually not so sure about that, after all. Had Brandon's belief in her spurred her on? Maybe. Being in a supportive, happy relationship had done wonders for her and had absolutely boosted her self-confidence. Regardless, Brandon should have known she wouldn't want his truckload of ready cash. He knew she was independent and believed in working hard for what she had and what she got. His grand gesture was about *him*, she realized. Not her. He was able to throw his money around and had.

As she opened her car door, Cornelius Taylor was coming out of the grand house, a tablet in his hand. Tall and imposing, he wore a leather vest over a Western shirt and dark jeans and boots.

He didn't even glance over to see who'd arrived. She rolled her eyes. The MO of someone who didn't have to care who'd arrived. He had people to care.

She got out and walked up to him. "Mr. Taylor, nice to see you again."

He finally looked up. "Miss Ware!" He clasped both her hands. "As mother of my future grand-heir, I'm thrilled to welcome you to the Taylor Ranch. Congratulations, by the way. Jessica and I are thrilled. This will be her first stepgrandbaby."

Cassidy smiled. Huh. She wasn't expecting him to be this effusive. He seemed a lot less scary. "I'm thrilled, too. Due in the springtime."

"Fabulous. I can envision an outdoor nursery in the backyard. I'll have our architect look into that. That little one will want for nothing. Now, as some-one who doesn't have any people, you don't have to worry. Did you know you can special order a handcrafted marble crib with an inset of diamonds in the shape of cows? Jessica found that on a baby website. We can use the Taylor Beef logo itself. You and Jessica can discuss all that on Saturday."

"People?" she repeated, stuck on that and grate-ful since she'd heard the words *cow-shaped dia-monds* and couldn't process *that*.

"Family. You're all alone. But not anymore. You're a Taylor now because of my grandheir. You make a list of what you need now and for when the baby comes, give it to Brandon and we'll get going on it. Jessica suggested a separate playroom in the house you build. We're thinking a wading pool, ball pit, climbing equipment, a children's library and art area. We'll have the playroom staffed with qualified childcare associates, of course." His phone rang and he glanced at it, giving her a moment to breathe.

Whoa. A little overbearing there, Mr. Taylor.

"Is Brandon here?" she asked as he typed something onto the tablet with two fingers. "I need to discuss something with him."

"In his home office," he said, still typing. "Make a left at the entry, second door on the right."

"Thanks," she called as she headed for the steps.

The house never failed to take her breath. Like a luxe log mansion, it stretched on forever, the mountains in the distance, the rustic landscape surrounding it so gorgeous and peaceful. She went inside, stopping and slowly turning, taking in the grand scale of the foyer alone, all polished wood and beams that managed to look rustic. The house reminded her of photos she'd seen of luxury guest ranches—the massive stone fireplace and the natural furnishings that made you feel as though you were in the wilds of Montana and a luxe spa at the same time.

She went down the long hall and came to the second door on the right.

Her anger came rushing back. It wasn't only that he'd assumed she needed him to achieve her goals. It was also the insane amount. Five hundred thousand dollars. As if that were nothing to him! *Oh,*

here's half a mil, Cassidy. Have fun with it, honey.
She shook her head. The arrogance!

Indoor wading pool. Qualified childcare associates in her baby's playroom! It was all too much for her to even digest.

Cassidy sucked in a breath, lifted her chin and knocked—hard.

"Come on in," Brandon called.

Cassidy opened the door and he looked up from where he sat at his desk, surprise lighting his handsome face.

She walked in, stopping halfway between the door and his huge desk. "I went to my bank today with my business plan to discuss my loan application for a new location in Lewistown," she said. "To my surprise, the loan officer told me I didn't need the paltry amount I asked for because I had a cool half million ready to be transferred into my account. All I had to do was sign."

He stood and came around the desk, half sitting against it. He was studying her, and could clearly see that she wasn't grateful. "I did want to surprise you. I figured when you were ready to open the second location, whenever that would be, it meant you believed in yourself and your business plan, and I wanted the money to be at your disposal whether that was now or another five years from now. *I* believe in you, Cassidy. Always have, always will."

Damn it. Why did he have to explain it that way, which tempered her anger. He was still in the wrong, but he'd acted from a place of kindness, not arrogance.

"Brandon, I don't want your funding. If I meet my goal to expand, it'll be on my own merit, with my own money—or borrowed money from my bank because *they* trust in my company and my business plan. So thank you, but no thank you."

He stared at her—and almost looked a bit hurt. "I admire you for that. But Cassidy, you're forgetting one thing. You're going to be the mother of my child. My money is your money."

No, you're forgetting one thing, Brandon. "We're not married, remember?" She closed her eyes, wishing she hadn't said that.

"Is that what you want?" he asked.

"Not with how things have been between us," she said, the emotion in her voice making her wince. "You're the one who wanted to get married—but your way. The loveless way. The cold, emotionless way. I can't and won't do that. But marriage isn't what I'm here about. I'm here about the money you arranged for me at my bank."

He glanced down for a moment, then back up at her. "I never want you to have financial issues, Cassidy. I never want money to come between you and your dreams. I *have* gobs of money. I want to share it with you. It's that simple." He turned and looked out the window.

She closed her eyes, shaking her head. He just didn't understand.

Or maybe she wasn't understanding him, not that she had to in this situation. But she had the feeling he was thinking about his mother. Looking for a huge payday and leaving her own children once she had it. But he quite obviously knew that Cassidy wasn't in any of this for the money.

"Brandon, I just want you to understand how important it is to me to make my own way. It's not that I don't appreciate what a generous person you are."

Cassidy heard footsteps and then Cornelius Taylor appeared in the doorway.

"Trust me, Miss Ware, *you* need the money," Cornelius said. "Take it as a safety net. Who the hell knows what will happen with you two? One day, you and Brandon likely won't be speaking to each other, and he'll have to pay you off anyway to keep our heir."

Cassidy gasped.

Brandon bolted up from where he'd been leaning against the desk, his expression angrier than Cassidy had ever seen. "Now you listen to me, Dad," he began, steam coming out of his ears.

"I most certainly will not," Cornelius said and huffed away.

"I'll deal with my father later," Brandon said to

her, his dark eyes glinting. "Mark my words. Right now, I want to finish our conversation."

"I said what I came to say." She waited, hoping *he'd* say something that would make everything okay again.

But he didn't say anything. She could see, plain as day on his face, that he wanted to. But he remained silent.

Cassidy turned and left, wishing he'd come after her, but she got to her car and he didn't appear in the doorway. *Fine. Whatever. I said my piece.*

She had no idea what was going to happen between them, where they'd go from here.

She only knew her heart was breaking.

When Cassidy left, Brandon thought about going after her, but he was still too furious at his father to think straight. He needed to clear his head before he could figure out how to make things right with her when everything was so wrong in so many ways. So he headed to the stables and got Starlight ready to go.

He passed the corrals and rode into the open land, his chest less tight, his head clearing the farther he went. The sun was setting, and the glare made it hard to see, but he was pretty sure a man who looked a lot like his brother Jordan was standing in front of a big, weirdly shaped rock by the creek. He rode over and, the closer he got, he was shocked to see it *was* Jordan, a mare grazing nearby. What the hell was he doing all the way out here?

Jordan turned at the approach, his gold wedding band glinting in the setting sun. Jordan and Camilla had recently returned from their honeymoon, both tanned and looking very happy whenever Brandon ran into them. His brother held a chamois cloth in one hand and a plastic container of something in the other. "Got in a fight with Dad?"

Brandon gave a bitter chuckle. "You know it." He peered closer at the big rock that Jordan had been facing. Wait a minute. He hopped off Starlight and moved closer to the rock. It was a heart. What? The rock, made from granite, was around two feet in circumference. It had to have been huge before someone had gone at it with a circular saw. "What's this?"

"Just something I've been doing when I get into it with Dad," Jordan said, rubbing it down with the cloth. "When Camilla and I were…trying to make it work, we came riding out here once, and we had a moment right at this spot, sitting on this rock, that turned my head around. So I wanted to immortalize it for Camilla. It's finished and I'll show it to her this weekend. I was just giving it a final polish."

"Damn. That's romantic."

"And practical," Jordan said. "Every time I ride

out here and see my heart, I know where my priorities are."

Man, had Jordan changed. But Brandon was too caught up in the word *priorities* to focus on his brother. *Brandon's* priority was the baby. He had to remember that. His relationship with Cassidy was up there, yes. But a relationship that would enable him to be a good father. Not a bitter angry one arguing about who disappointed whom.

Except you want that relationship to include sex. That's the opposite of platonic.

He sighed inwardly. He was a spoiled rich guy who wanted it both ways. And Cassidy wasn't about to give in to that. That was another reason he admired her so much.

But that didn't change how he *felt*.

"This party on Saturday…" Brandon said. "It's where I was going to announce that I'm about to become a father. Cassidy Ware is pregnant. I'll be a dad next spring."

Jordan's mouth dropped open. "Holy hell, Brandon. Congratulations." He pulled Brandon into a bear hug.

"Things are a little…rough right now."

"Ah," Jordan said, "in that case, find or make your own priority rock, whatever that may be. It'll help."

Brandon stared at the rock. His mind was going in so many directions, he wasn't really homing in on what his brother was saying. "I need to keep riding."

Jordan nodded. "That helps, too."

Yeah, it always did. Except this time, Brandon would have to ride for hours and he wasn't sure he'd ever find his answers.

Chapter Fifteen

Cassidy spent the rest of the week baking, working at Java and Juice, reading the book on motherhood she'd bought and keeping to herself. She'd avoided the sweet little book—wisdom and quotes for the new mother—that Brandon had bought her. It reminded her too much of how thoughtful he could be. He'd texted on Tuesday night that he was sorry how they'd left things and that he needed to take some time to think, to let things settle.

Fine with her. And not. Things had been so up and down with Brandon after such a whirlwind of heaven that she couldn't have taken any more of it. She needed to know where they stood so that she could know what her future was: with Brandon at her side or as a single mother with joint custody.

Now, on Friday morning, a new text came from him.

My dad's been avoiding me, easier than it sounds given we live in the same house. I'll be going to the party to confront him—privately. I'd like you to be there so that we can announce our news to the rest of the family together.

How warm and fuzzy, she thought, shaking her head. What a lovely invitation. She felt so much more comfortable. Not!

This is a family matter and I'm not family. We also need to talk and I don't intend to do that in earshot of your father ever again.

His response was quick.

Touché. But please. It's important to me that you're there.

She almost typed back a *why*, because she honestly had no idea. But she couldn't do this right now, couldn't handle texting back and forth when everything they had to talk about was so important. Fridays were always super busy at Java and

Juice. There was already a line of customers and she was also expecting to hear from the loan officer at the bank. *Focus on where you are*, she told herself. *Not your up-and-down romance.* Were they even a couple anymore? They were *something*—the baby on the way ensured that.

I'll be there. I'll drive myself so I can easily escape, if need be.

Touché, again, he texted back.

She'd made what seemed like a thousand complicated coffee drinks and plated pastry after pastry, ringing up snack and lunch orders when her phone pinged again.

This time it wasn't Brandon. She didn't recognize the cell phone number, but she did recognize the words.

You'll be glad you did it.

Oh, Winona, she thought, her heart all over the place. *Whatever it is I'm gonna do, I sure hope so.*

Because the family room at the Taylor Ranch was so huge, Brandon hadn't gotten near enough to his dad to demand an apology Cornelius would likely not give. As he'd told Cassidy yesterday via text, he'd do that privately. Jordan and Camilla were by the bar, Dirk and Dustin were chatting with all three of their uncles, and Cornelius and Jessica were deep in conversation. His father was throwing up his hands a lot. The two might be talking about the fact that Daphne was due to arrive any moment—or about the big blowup with Brandon and Cassidy, what Cornelius had said to her. That was, if his father even talked to Jessica about down-and-dirty stuff. Who knew what their relationship was really like. Maybe it was all superficial.

Jessica was much younger than Cornelius, but she truly seemed to like him. She was affectionate in a way that seemed natural and not forced. Brandon thought back to catching the couple dancing to a Blake Shelton tune. There was real romance in that dance; Brandon had seen it with his own eyes.

Part of him wanted to talk to his father about that, how Cornelius had found this third chance at love with Jessica when his first two marriages had collapsed. Heck, maybe he'd talk to Jessica about it. Even though they lived in the same house, albeit huge, they didn't see much of each other. Brandon should work on that. Spend more time with Jessica, especially now that she was going to be a grandmother to his child. He wondered if Jessica would open up about her marriage—not the details, but enough for Brandon to get a real sense about the depth of his stepmother's feelings for his blustery father—and his for her.

His father wasn't one to talk about marriage except to wave his hands around dramatically. Cornelius didn't talk much about Dirk and Dustin's mother, and he rarely talked about his first wife, Jordan, Brandon and Daphne's mother.

Speak of the devil. Daphne and Evan walked into the family room. He only thought of *Daphne* and *devil* in the same sentence because she'd gotten his head so turned around when he'd stopped by Happy Hearts to invite her to this party. Fighting against love. Please. He hadn't let himself get there in the first place. He didn't *love*. He *cared*. There was a difference.

He watched his father eye Daphne, the man's gaze moving to Evan. Cornelius whispered something to his wife then crossed the room to talk to his brothers. Brandon picked up his glass of wine and took a good long sip, then went to greet his sister.

He shook hands with Evan and hugged Daphne. "Party's a real blast," Brandon said. "I should tell you, Dad and I are on the outs, so I don't know how festive this evening will be."

Daphne nodded. "Well, festive and Dad aren't really a thing, so it's business as usual."

As she and her fiancé crossed the room to the bar, Brandon's gaze was drawn to the open

French doors and the beautiful woman who had just walked in.

Oh, Cassidy. Her blond hair was loose past her shoulders. She wore a floral black dress that swished around her knees and black cowboy boots. He'd missed her so much.

He walked over to her and wanted to envelop her in a hug, but her expression kept him from touching her. She was wary. With every reason.

"Ah! Everyone's here!" bellowed Cornelius Taylor's voice. "I'll make this short and sweet. Thanks to Brandon, Taylor Beef has scored rodeo champion Geoff Burris to star in the ad campaign, a particular boon ahead of the rodeo in November. Eat that, Abernathy Meats!"

Brandon's uncles clapped and laughed uproariously.

His father held up his glass of champagne. "To Brandon. To Taylor Beef! To Geoff Burris!"

Everyone turned toward Brandon and held up their glass then drank. Brandon downed his. Cassidy was sipping ginger ale.

Cornelius cleared his throat. "I'd also like to say that I'm glad Daphne is here with her fiancé, Evan Cruise. I may not always show it the best way, but you are family, Daphne. Sell that ridiculous Hoofy Hearts, have a steak, and you'll be welcomed back to the family with open arms." He raised his glass again, his eyes on his daughter.

If looks could maim, Cornelius Taylor would be flat on his back.

Daphne glared at him. "I will not drink to that. But I will toast to my brother's success in landing Geoff Burris. That's a major feat. Despite my leanings, I'm very much invested in the success of my siblings. Now, if you'll excuse me, Evan and I are out of here."

Cornelius scowled. Jessica had an *Oh dear* expression.

Jordan and Camilla were shaking their heads.

Dirk and Dustin were on their phones, probably also making plans to get away.

Cassidy was sort of nodding, as though this was expected. As if everything she'd been through with Cornelius made perfect sense.

"Now you listen to me, Cornelius Taylor," Cassidy suddenly said. Everyone stopped what they were doing and stared at her. "If you think I'm going to raise my child, your 'grandheir' as you refer to him or her, in this kind of intolerance for family, you have another think coming. I may not have money. I may not have people. But I have my values. Family should be everything. You have no idea how lucky you are, Mr. Taylor." With that, she turned and walked out.

The room erupted in claps and wolf whistles. Brandon heard his brother Dirk say to Dustin, "Wait, Cassidy is pregnant?"

Cornelius stood glowering, his arms across his chest. Jessica stared at her husband, her *Oh dear* expression morphed into something a little more hardcore. Maybe she'd try to talk some sense into her husband.

"Woman after my own heart," Camilla Sanchez Taylor whispered to Brandon. "I had a moment just like that with my father-in-law before Jordan and I got married. Not sure it got through. But it felt good. You tell Cassidy she's one hundred percent right."

Brandon squeezed Camilla's hand and took off through the French doors, hoping to catch Cassidy before she drove off.

He did. She stood with her hands at her sides then paced, as if trying to calm down before getting in her car.

"Cassidy," he called.

"Guess I'll never be invited back," she said, throwing up her hands. "Not that I want to be. But these are my baby's relatives. Your father is my baby's grandpa. I can't avoid that the way your father avoids your sister. Family *is* everything."

"I know," he said. "And I'm sorry you were put in that position. But I'm glad you spoke your mind. Camilla did that, too, before she married Jordan. She said to tell you you're a hundred percent right."

She stared at him. Hard. Studying him. She looked so beautiful in the moonlight, so equally strong and vulnerable, that he just wanted to gather her to him and hold her—and not let her go.

"Well, here's what I want to know, Brandon. Are *you* one hundred percent in? None of this 'one foot in, one foot out' bull. Are we together?"

He looked at the stars for a moment then back at Cassidy. "I…" He tried to find the words to explain how much she meant to him, but that the brick wall around his heart was impenetrable. He'd been through too much, seen too much. He wanted her in his life, but on his terms. And he wasn't even sure what those terms were.

"I love you, Brandon Taylor. Deeply. Can you say the same?"

Love. That word almost made him physically ill.

He could barely look at her. He tried to force himself, but he couldn't. *Don't love me*, he wanted to say. *I don't know how to love back. Even Winona said so, and she knows what she's talking about.*

"If we can have that platonic marriage, we can have it all," he said, knowing he sounded insane. "A united team for our child. Parents who care about each other, in the same house, with a shared goal of raising their kid together, putting the child first. Neither of us will miss anything. I know it's not exactly what you want, Cassidy, but it's a compromise, isn't it? Marriage is about a lasting partnership, making a relationship work. We can do that."

"You really don't see it, do you?" she asked.

"See what?" He didn't want to know, though.

"How like your father you really are. You believe in everything he said to me in your office the other day, Brandon. That one day we won't be speaking to each other. That you'll probably have to pay me off to keep your child. You actually *believe* that. It informs everything you do and controls you. It's *why* you can't love."

Red-hot anger swirled in his gut, but it was tamped by what felt like cold dirt being kicked up inside him. He didn't want to have this conversation. He couldn't.

"Goodbye, Brandon," Cassidy said, sounding so sad, but so firm. "We'll work out a schedule for the baby. We'll keep things friendly for his or her sake. But goodbye." With that, she ran to her car.

No. No, no, no. "Cassidy," he called, but he couldn't even hear himself. His voice was clogged with emotion.

He heard her car start, saw the lights come on.

She drove off, fast, leaving him standing there feeling like absolute hell.

The cramping started the next morning, when Cassidy should have been getting out of bed for an early morning of baking. But the pains low in her belly were too intense. She turned onto her other side.

Oh God. What was this? She was barely a month

along. She'd conceived the first week of September and now it was the last week. These couldn't be contractions.

A cold rush of fear gripped her. *Please, please, please, let everything be okay.* Please.

She grabbed her phone and called Brandon. Brandon—whom she'd said goodbye to last night.

"Cassidy?"

"My belly," she managed to blurt out between breaths. "It hurts so bad, Brandon."

"I'll be right there," he said, the desperation in his voice matching her own. "You stay on the phone with me." She could hear him moving, a door shutting, another door shutting, his truck starting. "I'm on my way. I'll be there in five minutes. Should I call an ambulance?"

Breathe, breathe, breathe, she told herself. "I don't think so. I just need to get to the hospital."

"I'm getting closer and closer," he said every minute as he drove, till he reached her apartment. "I'm here. I'm coming up. Can you unlock the front door for me?"

"I'll try," she said, getting out bed, doubled over, one hand on her belly as she staggered to the intercom to buzz him in and then unlocked the door. She turned and dropped onto the overstuffed chair that had been her mother's favorite.

The pains were getting worse.

"I'm coming up the stairs now," he said and then

burst into her apartment, putting his phone in his pocket.

She could see the worry and fear on his face. But she could only focus on the pain and trying to breathe through it.

Please let my baby be okay, she prayed with all her might.

Panicked, Brandon got Cassidy downstairs and to Bronco Valley Hospital as fast as he could without driving recklessly. When she was wheeled down the hall and out of sight, his heart split in two, half going with her.

He paced the waiting room, texting Daphne what was going on. Within fifteen minutes, his entire family was there, including his father and Jessica. He told the group what he knew, which was absolutely nothing. A nurse had told him the doctor would be out to talk to him when he finished his full examination of the patient.

Brandon paced some more then dropped into a chair, his forearms resting on his knees, his head down.

"Money poisoned my two marriages," Cornelius whispered when he sat beside Brandon. Or whispered as much as Cornelius Taylor's naturally booming voice *could* whisper. "I don't know a soul who'd turn down half a million dollars to make it on her own merit. That's a woman you should

MELISSA SENATE   271

marry, Brandon. And not because it would make good business sense, though it does, but because that woman is one in a million."

Brandon looked at his dad, the clog in his chest clearing somewhat. He hadn't realized how much the strife with his father had bothered him until his father just undid it.

"Jessica made me go to a couples workshop not too long ago, and I learned about projection," Cornelius added. "I realized on the way over that I was doing just that to you and Cassidy. Projecting. Just because my first two marriages didn't work out doesn't mean yours won't."

Brandon straightened and turned toward his dad. "I appreciate that." He'd appreciate it more if he wasn't so worried about Cassidy. He'd also be more focused on the fact that his dad went to a couples workshop.

"You love that woman," Cornelius said. "Like I love Jessica, God help me." He turned to look at his wife, who sat across the room, talking to Dirk and Dustin.

The air whooshed out of Brandon. He'd known in the Lewistown B and B that his feelings for Cassidy had gone rogue and were beyond his control. His subconscious must have been working behind the scenes the past days to keep him held back just enough. Self-preservation.

But now? All he could think about was Cassidy.

Cassidy and his baby. If he had to punch himself in the head to wake the hell up about what was important, he'd do it.

Actually, Cassidy walking away last night had done that. Knocked him upside the head.

"I do," Brandon said, realizing he'd lost the fight against love. He'd tried and failed spectacularly and for that he was grateful. It shouldn't have taken an emergency to conk him over the head and free his heart, but it had. And now he knew the truth. "I love her very much."

I love you, Cassidy Ware! He wanted to jump on his chair and scream it for everyone to hear. *I love you!*

"Told ya," Daphne whispered as she walked by, stopping to give his hand a squeeze. She nodded at Cornelius, her expression deservedly hard on the man, but still acknowledging their dad had done something right here.

Poor Brandon. Madly in love and fighting like hell against it.

What he needed right now was for Cassidy to be okay. For their baby to be okay. His baby was his priority rock, he knew, his brother's words coming back to him. *Find or make your own priority rock... It'll help.*

Actually, the baby alone wasn't his priority rock. Cassidy was, too. They both were. He loved them both. Cassidy because of the woman she was. The baby because he was Brandon's child. And when he met that child this spring, Brandon would love him for who he was, as well.

Understanding slammed into his head and his heart with such force that he almost tipped over.

He *did* love Cassidy. Madly. But he had a terrible feeling that he'd come to that realization too late.

Chapter Sixteen

Cassidy knew Brandon had to be sick with worry. Over an hour had passed since she'd arrived at the hospital, waiting, filling out forms, getting poked and prodded. She was fine. *The baby was fine.*

The moment she'd heard those words from the doctor she'd known that nothing else would matter as much. She would be okay.

With or without Brandon Taylor.

Her heart was broken, but her baby was just fine. And for that, she would be forever grateful.

The doctor had just signed her discharge papers, and as soon as she could get out of this hospital gown and into her clothes, she could leave.

According to a nurse, the waiting area was full of Taylors, one in particular who'd been pacing and constantly asking about her and the baby's condition.

That Brandon cared wasn't at issue. Of course he cared. But caring and loving were two different things.

A knock came on the door, and Cassidy called out for the person to come in. Brandon appeared, his face ashen, his dark eyes worried.

Her heart squeezed in her chest. How she loved this man. How was she supposed to let him go?

"Please tell me everything's okay, Cass," he said, sitting on the bed and taking her hands. "No one would tell me anything."

"The baby and I are both fine. The doctor ran tests. All is well. He said it was just some natural cramping, but that it's good I came in to be checked out. I have my discharge papers so I'm good to go once I get dressed."

She could see the relief hit him—so hard that he dropped his head in her lap.

He sat up straight and looked at her. "Cassidy, I have so much to say. So much to tell you."

"Oh yeah?" she asked. More of the same, she was sure. *Sorry. Sorry. Sorry. I can't. I can't. I can't.* Tears stung the backs of her eyes.

He nodded. "Yeah."

"Not here. Not while I'm in this bed and in this dumb backless gown. I want to go home."

"I'll give you some privacy to get dressed," he said. "My family's outside. They may mob you. My dad included. I'll let them know you're okay and they should go to give you space."

"I appreciate that," she said. She wasn't a part of that family. Her baby would be.

But not her.

He left and she let out a haggard, heartbroken sigh, then quickly got dressed. She waited a solid ten minutes before peeking outside. The Taylors were gone. Only Brandon remained.

He was quiet on the way to her apartment, quiet as he gently helped her up the stairs.

When the door closed behind him, she crossed her arms over her chest.

"Okay, I'm listening, Brandon."

Go ahead. Break my heart all over again.

Somehow, she was going to have to accept that he didn't love her, couldn't love, wouldn't love her.

She sat down on the sofa. He sat beside her and took both her hands, his eyes serious on hers.

"I'm so sorry about last night, Cassidy. You asked me if I loved you, and I didn't respond, like a total fool, but the truth is, I love you more than anything in the world. You mean everything to me. You and our baby. I love you so much. So, so much."

She stared at him. Everything she'd wanted him to say last night he was saying now. A few hours and a scare made that much difference?

She wasn't buying it. He *cared*. He'd been very afraid for her and the baby just an hour ago. But he didn't love her.

"That's the fear talking, I guess, Brandon. You were afraid you'd lose me or the baby and realized how much you care about both of us. That's a beautiful thing. But it's not love."

He gaped at her.

"Brandon, tonight, tomorrow, you'll realize what I'm saying is true."

"Now who doesn't want to believe the truth because she's scared?" he said softly. "I deserve not to be believed, Cassidy. You're right to be wary. And yeah, you scared the hell out of me. But I knew in Lewistown while sitting next to you in that baby seminar that I loved you like crazy."

"Lewistown?" she repeated. She remembered how he'd said he'd try. How he'd made love to her at the B and B. Like a man in love. Like a man who'd never let her go. That night, she'd believed in him, in them. That they really had a chance.

"I love you, Cassidy. You. And I love our baby-to-be. I will spend the rest of my life showing you how much."

She gasped. She could see the sincerity in his

eyes, in his expression. She felt it in his hands. "You do love me. You really do."

He moved the coffee table back a bit and then got down on one knee. "The ring is coming, Cassidy. But will you marry me? Will you make me the happiest man on this planet?"

Her eyes brimmed with tears. *Oh, Brandon.* "I will marry you. Yes, yes, yes!" she screamed.

He grinned and stood up and scooped her into his arms and kissed her. "I love you, Cassidy Ware."

"Guess we're not going our separate ways forever," she said with a smile.

"No, in fact, I want to marry you as soon as possible. Not because of the baby. Because of *you.* Oh, and my dad helped knock some sense into me. He said you were one in a million, and he's right."

"Speaking of millions… Well, a *tenth* of that, I got my loan. The bank officer left a message for me last night."

"Congratulations!" he said "I had nothing to do with that. I swear," he said, pressing a hand to his heart.

"I know," she said. "The loan officer assured me of that."

"I'm sorry I was so stubborn. That I fought against us. I'm so grateful to you for sticking by me, Cassidy."

She gasped again. "I'm glad I did it," she said

slowly. "That's it! That's what Winona knew I'd be glad that I did. Not give up on you. I knew my goodbye last night wasn't permanent. It never could be. We have a baby between us. I believed at the very beginning that you'd come around, and you did."

"I love you with all my heart," Brandon said, then kissed her again.

"We kissed and made up and it turns out we're staying together forever. Take that, fifteen-year-old bet."

He smiled. "Can I call the Taylors with the good news? I'll start with my Dad and Jessica."

"Go right ahead. Put them on speaker."

A few minutes later, there was whooping and wolf whistles, Cornelius and Jessica talking over each other in their excitement, yelling for Dirk and Dustin to come hear the great news.

"We all bought out the hospital gift shop," Cornelius said. "Lots of flowers, balloons and stuffed animals await you two. Sorry, but a quarter of it won't fit in that tiny apartment of yours. Guess we'll be seeing you around the ranch?"

Cassidy laughed. She and Cornelius would find their way. And she couldn't wait to get to know Jessica better. All the Taylors.

Cassidy Taylor. She liked the sound of it.

Finally, it was just the two of them again.

"Selfie of this special moment," Brandon said,

getting out his phone. "I'm going to send the photo to the family."

"You're going to be a great dad—and a great husband."

He hugged her, then held out the phone and snapped a photo, their smiles big like the love in their hearts.

Brandon grinned at the selfie. "You, me and our baby. Our family. Now I really know the meaning of the word *priceless*."

"Love you, Brandon Taylor."

"Love you times a million, Cassidy Ware Taylor to-be."

This time, she had no doubts of that.

Priceless, indeed.

* * * * *

Look for the next book in the new
Harlequin Special Edition continuity
Montana Mavericks:

The Real Cowboys of Bronco Heights
Grand-Prize Cowboy
by Heatherly Bell

On sale October 2021 wherever
Harlequin books and ebooks are sold.

And catch up with the previous
Montana Mavericks titles:

The Rancher's Summer Secret
by New York Times *bestselling author*
Christine Rimmer

For His Daughter's Sake
by USA TODAY *bestselling author*
Stella Bagwell

Available now!

COMING NEXT MONTH FROM

(H) HARLEQUIN

SPECIAL EDITION

#2863 A RANCHER'S TOUCH
Return to the Double C • by Allison Leigh

Rosalind Pastore is starting over: new town, new career, new lease on life. And when she buys a dog grooming business, she gets a new neighbor in gruff rancher Trace Powell. Does giving in to their feelings mean a chance to heal...or will Ros's old life come back to haunt her?

#2864 GRAND-PRIZE COWBOY
Montana Mavericks: The Real Cowboys of Bronco Heights
by Heatherly Bell

Rancher Boone Dalton has felt like an outsider in Bronco Heights ever since his family moved to town. When a prank lands him a makeover with Sofia Sanchez, he's determined to say "Hell no!" Sofia is planning a life beyond Bronco Heights, and she's not looking for a forever cowboy. But what if her heart is telling her Boone might just be The One?

#2865 HER CHRISTMAS FUTURE
The Parent Portal • by Tara Taylor Quinn

Dr. Olivia Wainwright is the accomplished neonatologist she is today because she never wants another parent to feel the loss that she did. Her marriage never recovered, but one night with her ex-husband, Martin, leaves her fighting to save a pregnancy she never thought possible. Can Olivia and Martin heal the past and find family with this unexpected Christmas blessing?

#2866 THE LIGHTS ON KNOCKBRIDGE LANE
Garnet Run • by Roan Parrish

Raising a family was always Adam Mills' dream, although solo parenting and moving back to tiny Garnet Run certainly were not. Adam is doing his best to give his daughter the life she deserves—including accepting help from their new, reclusive neighbor Wes Mobray to fulfill her Christmas wish...

#2867 A CHILD'S CHRISTMAS WISH
Home to Oak Hollow • by Makenna Lee

Eric McKnight's only priority is his disabled daughter's happiness. Her temporary nanny, Jenny Winslet, is eager to help make Lilly's Christmas wishes come true. She'll even teach grinchy Eric how to do the season right! It isn't long before visions of family dance in Eric's head. But when Jenny leaves them for New York City... there's still one Christmas wish he has yet to fulfill.

#2868 RECIPE FOR A HOMECOMING
The Stirling Ranch • by Sabrina York

To heal from her abusive marriage, Veronica James returns to her grandmother's bookshop. But she has to steel her heart against the charms of her first love, rancher Mark Stirling. He's never stopped longing for a second chance with the girl who got away—but when their "friends with benefits" deal reveals emotions that run deep, Mark is determined to convince Veronica they're the perfect blend.

HSECNM0921

*Raising a family was always Adam Mills' dream,
although solo parenting and moving back to tiny
Garnet Run certainly were not. Adam is doing his best
to give his daughter the life she deserves—including
accepting help from their new, reclusive neighbor
Wes Mobray to fulfill her Christmas wish…*

Read on for a sneak peek at
The Lights on Knockbridge Lane,
*the next book in the Garnet Run series and
Roan Parrish's Harlequin Special Edition debut!*

Adam and Wes looked at each other and Adam felt like
Wes could see right through him.

"You don't have to," Adam said. "I just… I accidentally
promised Gus the biggest Christmas light display in the
world and, uh…"

Every time he said it out loud, it sounded more
unrealistic than the last.

Wes raised an eyebrow but said nothing. He kept
looking at Adam like there was a mystery he was trying
to solve.

"Wes!" Gus' voice sounded more distant. "Can I touch
this snake?"

"Oh god, I'm sorry," Adam said. Then the words
registered, and panic ripped through him. "Wait, snake?"

"She's not poisonous. Don't worry."

That was actually not what Adam's reaction had been in response to, but he made himself nod calmly.

"Good, good."

"Are you coming in, or…?"

"Oh, nah, I'll just wait here," Adam said extremely casually. "Don't mind me. Yep. Fresh air. I'll just… Uh-huh, here's great."

Wes smiled for the first time and it was like nothing Adam had ever seen.

His face lit with tender humor, eyes crinkling at the corners and full lips parting to reveal charmingly crooked teeth. Damn, he was beautiful.

"Wes, Wes!" Gus ran up behind him and skidded to a halt inches before she would've slammed into him. "Can I?"

"You can touch her while I get the ladder," Wes said.

Gus turned to Adam.

"Daddy, do you wanna touch the snake? She's so cool."

Adam's skin crawled.

"Nope, you go ahead."

Don't miss
The Lights on Knockbridge Lane
by Roan Parrish, available October 2021 wherever Harlequin Special Edition books and ebooks are sold.

Harlequin.com